WITNESS PROTECTION UNRAVELED

MAGGIE K. BLACK

D0037350

LOVE INSPIRED SUSPENSE
INSPIRATIONAL ROMANCE

LOVE INSPIRED® SUSPENSE
INSPIRATIONAL ROMANCE

ISBN-13: 978-1-335-40279-0

Recycling programs
for this product may
not exist in your area.

Witness Protection Unraveled

This edition published by arrangement with Harlequin Books S.A.

For questions and comments about the quality of this book,
please contact us at CustomerService@Harlequin.com.

Love Inspired
22 Adelaide St. West, 40th Floor
Toronto, Ontario M5H 4E3, Canada
www.Harlequin.com

Printed in U.S.A.

Are not five sparrows sold for two farthings,
and not one of them is forgotten before God? But even
the very hairs of your head are all numbered. Fear not
therefore: ye are of more value than many sparrows.
–Luke 12:6-7

To all the found family who are now in my life
and all those who I have yet to find.

Especially my brother-friend-colleague George Luke
and his HEA, Karen.

A bang sounded from somewhere to her right. Jessica grabbed another door handle and threw it open.

And for the first time in years, laid eyes on Travis.

Her heart caught in her throat. Her former partner had his back up against the wall, with a handgun pointed to the side of his head. His attacker wore a bulky orange reflective jumpsuit and a creepy bug-like silver respirator mask.

Travis's dark brown eyes met hers over his attacker's shoulder, somehow looking so achingly familiar and yet completely new in ways she didn't have time to process.

Somehow she knew exactly what he wanted from her.

Not rescue, but a distraction.

She nodded. *I got it.*

"Hey, you! Stop!" She yanked her weapon from her ankle holster. "Right now! Drop your gun!"

The figure glanced toward her and Travis struck, knocking him sideways. The figure stumbled toward her. Then came the light—sharp, bright and blinding. A fist struck out.

"Jess!" She heard Travis's voice calling her name.

But she couldn't see where he was. She couldn't see anything at all.

Maggie K. Black is an award-winning journalist and romantic suspense author with an insatiable love of traveling the world. She has lived in the American South, Europe and the Middle East. She now makes her home in Canada with her history-teacher husband, their two beautiful girls and a small but mighty dog. Maggie enjoys connecting with her readers at maggiekblack.com.

Books by Maggie K. Black

Love Inspired Suspense

Protected Identities

Christmas Witness Protection
Runaway Witness
Witness Protection Unraveled

True North Heroes

Undercover Holiday Fiancée
The Littlest Target
Rescuing His Secret Child
Cold Case Secrets

Amish Witness Protection

Amish Hideout

Military K-9 Unit

Standing Fast

Visit the Author Profile page at Harlequin.com for more titles.

ONE

Travis Stone sprinted down Main Street in the small town of Kilpatrick, Ontario, ignoring the fact that Detective Jessica Eddington, the one and only woman his damaged heart had ever really cared about, was now relentlessly calling his cell phone.

The late June evening was warm around him. The air was thick with the threat of rain. He was fifteen minutes late to pick up the two most amazing little kids in the world, and their grandmother, Patricia, needed him to take them so she could close up her store for the night and rush off to her book club. Right now, that was what mattered.

When he'd gotten them from Patricia's and dropped them off at school in the morning, five-year-old Willow had told him she'd had a nightmare about a "shiny man" with a flashlight standing outside her bedroom window. Travis figured it was probably just part of her dealing with the tragic death of her police officer parents six months ago, shortly after Willow's baby brother was born. They'd both been killed when a drunk driver had panicked and accidentally careened through the impaired driving checkpoint they'd been manning. Still, not giving Willow or her grandmother any reason to worry mattered more right now than stopping long enough to take Jess's call.

Even if, after four long years hiding in witness protection, he still missed Jess so much that even just seeing his former partner's name on the screen made his chest ache to breathe.

Travis and Jess had worked over fifty cases together and, according to her message, Jess was calling to get his advice about one more for "old times' sake." Considering the dangerously unhealthy workaholic he'd once been, he didn't want to risk getting sucked back into the career that had almost destroyed him. Not one case. Not one call. Even though hearing her voice on his voice mail a few days ago had almost been enough to make him call her back to say he'd help with the case.

Lord, help me be strong enough to not get mixed up in whatever case Jess wants my help on and to put my life as a detective behind me forever.

The final operation he and Jess had worked together—taking down an international crime lord known only as "the Chimera"—had led to a disastrous personal failure that had forced Travis into witness protection for his own safety. It had felt like the death of everything he'd cared about but had led instead to his slow and painful rebirth as a new man in this close-knit Ontario community. He was now a better man. One who showed up for the people who mattered. One who didn't toss back coffee and caffeine drinks to stay awake all day and then pour obsessively over files or pace crime scenes at night like an irritable and jittery insomniac. He no longer laughed off belief in God or snapped at anyone who irritated him.

He was now a man people cared about and relied on. He couldn't give that up.

Not even for Jess. No matter how much her dazzling blue eyes and determined smile might still float at the edges of his mind some nights.

The phone stopped ringing as he passed Harris's Bakery. He waved a quick hand at the couple sitting on a bench by the front door. The new kindergarten teacher, Alvin Walker, had his arm around Harris Mitchell's daughter Cleo. That was new, and likely to be the most exciting gossip Kilpatrick had seen in weeks, especially since Cleo's last boyfriend, Braden, had been a particularly nasty piece of work.

"Hey, where's the fire?" Alvin shouted to him.

Three years since Travis had joined Kilpatrick's voluntary firefighter brigade and still the joke never got old.

"Got to pick up Willow and Dominic for dinner so Patricia can close up the store," Travis called without letting his footsteps falter. "And I'm running late!"

Alvin laughed. "Well, you'd better hurry then."

He was. Travis reached Tatlow's Used Books and Café with its tiny apartment on the second and third floor that Travis called home. The red and white sign in the front window had already been flipped to Closed but the front door was still unlocked. He pushed the door open, as chimes jingled.

"I'm here!" he called. "Sorry I'm late! Someone called the volunteer firefighters about a baby skunk caught in a smoothie cup. Took me forever to coax him out—"

He froze. The store was empty. No gray-haired Patricia wagging an understanding finger at him from behind the front desk. No Willow leaping up from a spot on the multicolored carpet where she'd been "reading" her baby brother a picture book and then charging into his arms. And yet the lights were on. Stained-glass lamps cast a gentle glow over an array of mismatched furniture, well-worn shelves stacked high with books and the long side counter that sold flavored coffees and pastries. An unexpected chill ran down his spine. Where was everyone?

"Patricia?" The front door swung shut behind him. "Willow?"

Then he heard a crack, soft and muffled like a firecracker going off inside a blanket, followed by the faint clink of something metal hitting the floor. No matter how many years he spent in civilian life, he'd never forget those sounds. Somewhere inside Tatlow's Used Books someone had fired a handgun with a silencer and the bullet casing had fallen to the floor.

I don't know what's going on here, Lord. But I need Your backup right now.

The undercover detective he'd once been knew without a doubt that if he didn't proceed cautiously he could put himself in the line of fire. But the man he was now—part-time landscaper, unexpected babysitter and volunteer firefighter—knew that he'd gladly take a bullet for Patricia and her grandchildren.

What had started out as a simple landlady and tenant situation when he'd first rented the apartment above the bookstore had found him unexpectedly blessed by a family. It had been Patricia's son and daughter-in-law, Geoff and Amber who'd practically hauled him through the rough patch of starting his life all over again, even though he'd never been able to tell them why he'd come to town and that he'd once also worn a badge. When Geoff and Amber had then been struck and killed, leaving elderly Patricia alone in the world and orphaning the children, Travis had vowed he'd do whatever it took to keep them safe. He wasn't about to break that promise now.

"Willow?" he shouted, scanning the main room rapid-fire before moving into the next one. "Anyone there? Shout if you can hear me!"

A crash sounded that seemed to shake the walls around him and his hand reached instinctively for the weapon he no longer carried. He made his way through the bookstore then pushed through a door into the back hallway. To his left was the staircase leading to his second-floor apartment. Straight ahead was the door that led outside. He turned right and ran into the back storeroom.

And saw his landlady's lavender-clad pant legs and sensible shoes sticking out from behind a pile of boxes.

"Patricia!" He dropped down on the floor by her side. "Are you okay? What happened? Where are the kids? I heard a gunshot."

Sweat soaked her short white hair and her face was pale, but he didn't see any obvious injuries or blood.

"Travis…" Her eyes were open but as she tried to sit, pain flooded her face. "I saw a bright light…and I… I think I fell…off the ladder."

Had she? A rolling ladder lay just a few feet away and he knew how stubborn she was about doing things herself instead of waiting for help.

"A light?" he repeated. "Like a gunshot or flash-light?"

Like the "shiny man" from Willow's nightmare? It had been just a nightmare, right? There hadn't actually been someone outside Patricia's remote farmhouse shin-ing a light in the little girl's window, had there?

"It was like…" Patricia's voice faltered. "Like a cam-era flash."

A portable video baby monitor lay on the floor by her side. The screen was shattered.

"Where are the children?" he asked again.

"Upstairs. Asleep."

He reached for his cell phone and dialed.

"Nine-one-one. What's your emergency?" The voice was male and crisp. Travis quickly gave him the address and the details. The dispatcher confirmed paramedics were on their way. His phone rang again but he ignored it as Patricia's eyes fluttered closed.

"The children are safe upstairs?" Travis repeated.

Patricia nodded faintly. "In your apartment. Domi-nic was napping and Willow fell asleep reading to him. I was watching them on the monitor."

"Okay," Travis said. He'd set up a few baby monitor screens around his apartment and the store, so the adults could be in another room while the kids napped. "Paramedics are on their way. I'm going to run next door and get someone to come wait with you while I go check on the kids."

He turned to go, but felt Patricia grab his hand. He spun back.

"Promise me you'll take care of my grandbabies," she said. There was a weight to her words he couldn't grasp. "No matter what. Promise me."

"Of course," he said. He squeezed her hand gently and let it go. "I promise."

Then he ran back outside as fast as he could push his legs to go. Seconds later, he was back with Alvin and Cleo, who'd immediately leaped to their feet and agreed to help. Once he was sure they were settled with Patricia, he pelted upstairs. He was almost at his apartment door when his phone rang again. This time he answered. "Hello?"

"Hey Travis? It's…Jess… Um, Detective Jessica Eddington." Instantly her face swept into his mind, her long blond hair tied up in a bun at the nape of her neck and her perceptive blue eyes on his face. "I know this is unexpected but—"

"Is this a secure line?" Travis cut her off before she could finish her sentence.

"Yes—"

"Has my witness protection file been compromised?" he asked.

"No," Jess said and he appreciated how direct her answer was.

"Are you sure?" he persisted. "Is there any way the Chimera knows I'm still alive?"

Known only by his alias, "the Chimera" was believed to be from Eastern Europe and had managed to amass a cruel and vicious international operation due to one simple principle: no one who'd ever seen his face or left his employ lived to talk about it. When Travis had gone undercover to take down his North American operation, with Jess as his behind-the-scenes partner, they'd successfully located and dismantled his cover business, arrested his entire team and freed every person he'd trafficked.

But one thing had gone disastrously wrong. They hadn't arrested the Chimera or successfully identified him. Yet Travis had seen his face. He'd even had the man set in his sights, but his hands had been shaking so hard from lack of sleep plus caffeine withdrawal, he'd failed to make the shot. No match had ever been made for the police sketch Travis had been able to supply. The Chimera had set a fifty-thousand-dollar bounty on his head, and the man Travis had once been had disappeared forever.

"We've had absolutely no indication of any kind that your identity has been compromised," Jess said.

"The entire RCMP witness protection database was stolen by criminal hackers at Christmas," Travis reminded her. "Over a dozen files were auctioned off."

"And your secret identity file wasn't one of them."

"Yeah, I know," Travis said. He'd fielded over half a dozen calls from RCMP officers in the months since then, both reassuring him of that fact and offering him a new identity if he wanted one. But he hadn't been about to leave Kilpatrick.

He reached the top of the stairs and unlocked his apartment door. "So you all say. But I'm dealing with a potential situation and I need to know if it could be connected to me, my past, my identity, criminals we took down together, the Chimera, any of it?"

There was a short pause, as if Jess was confirming something before responding. From the background noise, it sounded like she was in a car. When her voice came back, she was all cop.

"No," she said, "there has been absolutely no suspicious activity anywhere online related to you."

He breathed a prayer of thanksgiving.

"What's going on?" she asked.

Hopefully nothing.

"My landlady fell," he said. One of the two children he'd babysat might've seen a "shiny man" with a flashlight outside Patricia's farmhouse and mistaken it for a nightmare. And he was still really sure he'd heard a gunshot even if he didn't know where or how. "I gotta go. I'll call you later."

He hung up before Jess could answer, his heart still reeling from having heard the sound of her voice, and ran through his front door, down the hallway and into his study. Dominic's crib was empty as was the little cot beside it that Willow sometimes napped on. Warm June wind rushed through the open window that led out to the fire escape.

The floor creaked behind him. Travis felt a blow, swift and hard on the back of his head. He fell forward, dropping his phone as it rang. The last thing he saw before being jumped from behind was Jess's Caller ID.

Detective Jess Eddington stared down at her cell phone where it sat mounted on the dashboard of her car. Her hands shook as she tightened them on the steering wheel. Hearing Travis's warm and deep voice down the phone line had unexpectedly stirred something inside her, like how hearing a snatch of a song could take her back to a place and a time she'd loved long ago. She glanced up at the blue-and-white sign welcoming her to the town of Kilpatrick. Travis still had no idea she was here.

"Well, you tried to warn him we were coming." The lackadaisical voice of hacker Seth Miles rose from the seat beside her. He had two laptops balanced on his long, skinny legs plus at least two cell phones. "I can't believe he actually hung up on you. That's gotta sting. Remind me again why we drove six hours across the province to recruit a man for an operation who clearly doesn't want to talk to you?"

She pressed her lips together and drove. Seth was teasing her and she didn't have to rise to the bait. But that didn't stop the answer to his question from circling through her mind. Because she was about to take on the riskiest mission of her life to unmask the vicious crime lord who'd forced Travis into witness protection and didn't want to do it without him.

Travis had been one of the best she'd ever worked with, in the grueling and exhausting work of taking down those who preyed on the most vulnerable. While he'd worked too long hours and was frequently worn down from forgetting the basics like eating or sleeping, he'd also been relentless and thorough, and had this way of having her back that made her feel invincible.

The sheer relief and elation she'd felt four years ago when they'd finally taken down the Chimera's entire Canadian operation had led to heartbreak when somehow a fluke missed gunshot had led to the crime lord himself getting away and escaping the country, forcing Travis to fake his death and give up his life in law enforcement for good.

But things had changed since then. She'd been part of forming an elite, off-the-grid team that had worked hard to undo the damage of the theft and sale of the witness protection files. They'd gotten smarter about protecting people's identities and one of their own, Seth, was himself in witness protection. With the right tactics and new location, they could completely hide Travis from the Chimera, too, while he helped her stop him once and for all.

"Because we could use someone like Travis," she said eventually, trying and failing to keep her thoughts to herself. "He's the best I've ever worked with. He risked everything to take down the Chimera. We thought the crime lord had escaped the country and gone underground for good, until his name popped up in your dark web data analysis of the secret identity file auction. If I'm going to track the Chimera down and stop him for good this time, I need Travis. I know he can't ever go undercover again, but he can still be my handler back at headquarters with you."

Was she reminding herself? Reminding Seth? Or practicing out loud what she was going to say to Travis? When he hadn't replied to her voice mail, she'd assumed he might not think the phones were secure, and so had decided to come to him in person.

Everything had fallen into place with the Chimera operation at rapid speed. Seth had identified his cover operation as a holiday complex in Victoria three days ago. She'd applied for a job as a hostess the next day and was set to start her cover life there on Monday. Everything was in place. All she needed was Travis. She glanced to the clouds above and prayed he'd say yes. He just had to.

"Why are you so set on this guy when it's his fault your first mission against the Chimera failed?" Seth asked.

Something bristled at the back of her neck. "The mission didn't fail," she said. "The Chimera's entire operation was taken down, all of his henchmen went to jail and dozens of women he'd trafficked were freed."

"Travis's file says he had the Chimera in his sights and missed the shot."

"The file doesn't know him," Jess said. "I do. We worked fifty-two cases together."

"How did he miss the shot?" Seth asked.

"I don't know. I wasn't there." Which was a bit of a cop-out answer, considering she'd been in his earpiece at the time. "I didn't have eyes. The Chimera ran. Travis took the shot and missed. It could've happened to anyone."

Seth shrugged. "The file says it was officer error."

"And your file says you used to be a criminal," she shot back.

Seth snorted. "People change. Or so I've heard."

She knew he wasn't the slightest bit offended at being reminded of his past. Seth was like a duck that way. Everything rolled off his back. Yet she was slightly irked at his good-natured banter and wasn't sure why. She'd worked with Travis for years and had no doubt he'd beat himself up to no end about missing the shot. Besides, she was giving him a chance to redeem himself by finally taking the Chimera down for good.

"His file also says he racked up a whole lot of speeding tickets," Seth added.

She ignored him. Seth didn't say anything for a long moment. Instead the former criminal hacker now mostly reformed member of her team, kept typing away furiously on the laptop balanced on his knees. Then he frowned.

"Please, tell me we're heading straight to Tatlow's Used Books and Café," Seth said.

"Why?" she asked.

"Because I just picked up an ambulance dispatch to that location," Seth said. "Elderly woman, potential fall."

"Yeah, Travis had mentioned his landlady had an accident."

"Plus there's this." Seth pushed a button and a small child's voice filled the car.

"Maynaise. Maynaise." The voice was young and scared, but also very determined. "This is Willow Tatlow with my brother, Dominic. We're in Uncle Travis's apar'ment. Uncle Travis has been captured by the Shiny Man. Send rescue. Over."

Jess gasped. "What is that?"

The town ahead grew closer. Seth played the little girl's voice again on repeat.

"I don't know, that's all I've got," Seth said. "It sounds like she was sending it on a very short-wave radio signal and then changed to a different channel looking for a response. I'm guessing a walkie-talkie or baby monitor. Tell me you know what that was about."

"Not a word." She could see the bookstore ahead on her right now. An ambulance was parked by the front door and a small crowd had gathered. She pulled up a few doors down and watched as an elderly woman she recognized from her intel as Travis's landlady, Patricia Tatlow, was wheeled out the front door on a stretcher, flanked by a couple she didn't recognize. Her eyes were open, which Jess took as a good sign. A tall, winding fire escape crawled up one side of the building, facing the bakery next door. She glanced up. There were windows open on both the second and third floors.

"I'm going in," she said. "You're coming with me. So stash your computers and grab us both an earpiece." She yanked her long, blond hair free from its ponytail and shook her head so that it fell around her shoulders almost all the way to her waist. She didn't normally wear her hair down. At five foot two, with the type of eyes people sometimes called "baby blues," adding natural blond hair to the mix made people assume she was more of a peppy cheerleader than a veteran RCMP detective. Came in handy for hiding earpieces though.

"Need I remind you our entire plan was not to blow his cover," Seth said.

"I'm not going to blow his cover," Jess said, taking the earpiece the second it appeared in his hand. "We're going up the fire escape." Thankfully, Seth was tall enough to grab the bottom rung of the fire ladder and pull it down, so she wouldn't have to jump for it. "If anyone asks, I'm an old friend, you're my brother and we're coming to surprise him. Now, come on."

They exited the car and strode down the sidewalk, weaving their way through the gathered crowd and then slipping into the alley between the bookstore and bakery. Seth yanked the fire ladder down and they started up. The first second-floor window they reached opened into a kitchen. She glanced at Seth. "I'll take this floor, you take the third. Got it?"

Seth nodded and ran past her, his footsteps clanking as he went. She slid through the open window and entered a narrow kitchen. Two chairs, one with a booster seat, sat at a small table, along with a high chair. The wall was covered in pictures, taped up in every possible space. Most were colorful splattering and scrawling done no doubt by a child. But a few were more artistically sketched drawings of a woman with long, flowing, blond hair, her face completely turned away from the person drawing her. Jess felt her heart stutter a beat. Even without a face, the woman in the picture looked an awful lot like her.

Jess slid through the door and came out into a hallway. More doors stood to her left and there was a staircase to the third floor on her right.

"I've got the kids!" Seth's voice crackled in her ear. "They're safe."

Jess thanked God. She could hear a child's voice babbling in the background.

"Willow says she saw Uncle Travis on a monitor screen being attacked by the Shiny Man," Seth added.

"Just keep them safe," Jess said, "and hang tight."

A bang sounded from somewhere to her right. She ran back into the hall, grabbed another door handle and threw it open.

And, for the first time in years, laid eyes on Travis.

Her heart caught in her throat. Her former partner's back was up against the wall and there was a handgun pointed to his head. His attacker wore a bulky, orange-reflective jumpsuit, like a construction worker, work gloves and a creepy, buglike silver respirator mask with large bulbous filters on either side of his face.

The figure in reflective gear shouted at her in an electronically distorted voice that he'd put a bullet through Travis's head if she so much as moved.

Travis's dark brown eyes met hers over his attacker's shoulder, somehow looking so achingly familiar and yet completely new in ways she didn't have time to process. And as she read all the conflicting emotions flickering through his gaze, it was as if all the years they'd spent apart were ripped away like unwanted pages from a book.

Somehow she knew exactly what he wanted from her.

Not rescue, but a distraction.

She nodded. *I got it.*

Don't blow my cover. His eyes seemed to plead.
I won't.

"Hey, you! Stop!" She yanked her weapon from her ankle holster and held it up with both hands. "Right now! Drop your gun!"

The gunman glanced toward her and Travis struck, smashing his palm into the side of his face and knocking him sideways. The man stumbled toward her. Something small flickered in his other hand. Then came the light—sharp, bright and blinding—searing her eyes and robbing her of her vision. A fist struck out at her, catching her off guard and sending her stumbling.

"Jess!" She heard Travis's voice calling her name.

But she couldn't see where he was. She couldn't see anything at all.

TWO

The light was like nothing she'd ever experienced before, blinding her eyes so suddenly and completely that all she wanted to do was press her hands over them. Instead she closed them, tightly. Her heart pounded wildly as, for a moment she stumbled, fighting the urge to drop her weapon in case it misfired.

Then a pair of strong hands grabbed her shoulders and she felt herself being pulled into a muscular chest.

"It's okay, Jess." Travis's voice was in her ear, firm and reassuring. "Just breathe. I know it hurts and it's scary, but it'll pass. Now, I'm going to take the gun from you, just for safety's sake."

"Thanks." She let him take it. She didn't know how he knew that was what she'd been most worried about, only that somehow she knew what he'd be most worried about, too. "Willow and Dominic are safe upstairs with my colleague, Seth."

The long sigh of relief she felt move through his core told her she'd been right.

Then she heard him pray and thank God. Huh? The

Travis she used to know had given up on his faith long ago and used to roll his eyes whenever she'd prayed.

"How do we contact their parents?" she asked.

"Their parents are gone," Travis said. "They were friends of mine. Geoff and Amber Tatlow. Both cops. Amber went back to work part-time eight weeks after Dominic was born. They were both working at a roadside impaired driving checkpoint on the highway, just pulling drivers over to make sure nobody's drunk, over-tired or impaired, like cops do across the country every long weekend. One drunk driver apparently panicked and tried to drive around the road stop, injuring three people in the process and killing Geoff and Amber." She felt Travis shrug. "Their grandmother, Patricia, is all they have now."

And him apparently.

"I saw Patricia being rolled out on a stretcher and into an ambulance," Jess said. "She looked conscious. I think a man and woman got in the ambulance with her."

"That was probably Willow's new kindergarten teacher Alvin and the baker's daughter Cleo," Travis said, and there was something both coplike and familiar in how he was giving more detail than was necessary. "One of them will contact me as soon as there's news. They'll know I'm with the kids and Kilpatrick is the kind of town where people keep everyone else in the loop."

She heard him set her gun down on the desk. Then he wrapped his arms around her and held her tightly. She wasn't sure if the hug was because she'd been blinded or if he was happy to see her.

"You said there was no active threat against me," he said, an edge to his voice that belied the softness of his hug. "You said my identity hadn't been compromised."

"There wasn't," she said. "It hadn't."

"Are you sure?" he asked and, even with her eyes closed, she could sense him searching her face.

"Yes."

"Then how…why are you even here?"

"You weren't returning my calls," she said, "so my colleague Seth and I drove out to see you."

"The same Seth who's with Willow and Dominic now?" Travis asked.

It was bizarre. He was grilling her and holding her at the same time.

"Yes," she confirmed. "Seth Miles, the hacker. Remember hearing about him? He only hacked criminals, there was a warrant out for his arrest, he got hunted by really bad guys and then ended up in witness protection."

Travis blew out a long breath. Yeah, she wasn't surprised Travis remembered the man's name, considering the stir he'd made a few years back. Not that he probably had any idea who Seth had become since then.

"Now he's my team's tech guy," she said. "He's like an obsessive savant when it comes to all things online and he picked up a distress signal Willow sent through the baby monitor's short-wave."

"Whoa," Travis said.

She pulled back out of his arms slightly, tried opening her eyes and saw nothing but a wall of white swimming with indistinct dark shapes. She gritted her teeth.

So much for hoping she could do anything for a moment other than stand there helplessly and pray Travis was right about the light thing.

"Your turn," she said. "Who's the Shiny Man? Where did he go? What does he want? And what did he hit me with?"

"I don't know who he is or what he wants." Frustration filled Travis's voice. "He showed up when Patricia was closing the store, confronted her in some way and then ran upstairs where I found him. He went down the fire escape and he hit us both with some kind of high-brightness tactical flashlight. Illegal, I'm guessing, but temporary. His whole get up, from the reflective gear to the respirator mask, could've easily been slapped together from an online tactical gear store."

"So, probably not a pro. And much sloppier than anyone the Chimera would ever hire, so I expect there's no connection there." Jess opened her eyes again, thankful to see less white and more splotches. "But apparently the kind of criminal to plan ahead, considering he was in disguise. Did he steal anything?"

"No." Worry moved through Travis's voice. "My laptop and tablet computer are all still here, along with some emergency cash I had in a jar on my desk."

There was a matter-of-fact dryness to his tone. It was reassuring, and Jess suddenly realized how much she'd missed it. There'd often been a sharpness to his voice, too, that other people had thought of as rude. Maybe it had been a little intense, but she'd liked the fact it was direct and to the point. He'd never been one for compliments or affection. He'd never even hugged her, until now.

Travis stepped even further back, her hands slipping down his arms and coming to rest just below his elbows. She felt the strength of muscles under her fingertips. His chest had been unexpectedly strong, too.

The Travis she'd known hadn't exactly been weak but, with the exception of his time on undercover assignment, he'd definitely been a desk jockey. But this new Travis felt like he could fell trees with an ax. Her mind flickered back to the sketches of the woman on the kitchen wall. Was he now an artist, too?

She looked up into Travis's face and blinked as slowly it came into focus. His eyes were worried and his strong jaw was clenched. He reached for her hand and took it in his. While she knew it was only to guide her, somehow that didn't stop the warmth of his touch from spreading through her limbs. She tapped her earpiece to keep herself from focusing on it.

"Seth, I've got Travis. He was attacked by someone who got away by shining a tactical light in my eyes. How are the kids?"

"Good." Seth's voice came back in her ear. "I'm sitting in the playhouse, holding Dominic while Willow is telling me about all her favorite books. Apparently one of them has the cover on upside down."

"Willow really loves books," Travis said, and Jess realized he was leaning in close enough to pick up Seth's voice in her earpiece.

"We're on our way."

Travis picked up her gun, removed the clip and

helped her slide it back into her ankle holster. Then Travis straightened and took her hand. When she pulled it out of his grasp, he didn't question it. Her vision still wasn't great, but she'd rather use the walls for guidance if need be than be led around.

They walked out of his study and back into the hall-way.

"There's a lot of people gathered downstairs," Jess said as they started up the stairs to the third floor. "It's like the whole block turned out to make sure Patricia was okay."

Travis paused halfway up the stairs, as if a new thought had just hit him. "Please tell me you didn't blow my cover."

Jess shook her head. "No, we came up the fire escape. Though the Shiny Man might've heard you call me 'Jess' and definitely knows I was carrying a gun." Although she'd done her best not to sound like a cop when she'd pulled it.

They kept walking, reached the top of the stairs and entered a wide attic that had been converted into a living room with mismatched furniture and slanted ceilings cutting down in corners on all sides. An empty playpen sat beside a large window bow filled with pillows. A large pink-and-purple wooden playhouse, about four feet tall, stood against a wall on the far side of the room. The door was closed, but when Travis crouched in front of the playhouse door and knocked three times, it swung open.

Seth's six-foot form sat cross-legged and folded sideways on the floor, with a sleeping baby, about eight or nine months old, curled up in his arms. The baby's eyes were closed and he was sucking on a blue pacifier with a tiny yellow duck on it.

"You must be Seth," Travis said. "You look nothing like your reputation."

Seth snorted. "You don't much look like yours."

"Uncle Travis!" A small girl with long blond hair and huge green eyes crawled out from around Seth. She slipped from the playhouse and barreled into Travis's arms. "You escaped the Shiny Man!"

"Of course I did!" Travis swept her up into his arms as she clasped them around his neck. "There is nothing for you to be scared about, Willow. I will always keep you and Dominic safe. I promise. Your nan had a little fall, but she's going to the doctor's now and they'll take good care of her."

Willow took his face in her hands and turned it until he was looking directly into her eyes.

"I saw the Shiny Man outside my window at night with a flas'light," she said, seriously.

Travis nodded. "I know. And I'll make sure he never bothers you again."

Jess knew as he said the words that he had no idea how he was going to make good on his promise to the little girl, but that he'd do everything in his power to figure it out. She'd heard him make similar promises to victims they'd known only through photos or videos on their screens back when they'd worked special victims cases. And no matter what it had taken, how many hours he'd had to work, or what kind of evidence he'd needed to go through, Travis had always come through for them.

Willow's face spread into a wide and trusting smile. Unexpected tears rushed to the corners of Jess's eyes. Was it because she'd never imagined Travis as the kind of man who'd have a family? Or because it was rare in her line of work to see little children being so protected, cared for and loved?

A wail filled the air. The baby was awake. She glanced past Travis to Seth, who still sat holding Dominic like the little boy was a very fragile bomb he was working very hard to keep from exploding. She wondered if the hacker had ever even held a baby before. In a single, smooth and seamless motion, Travis shifted Willow into one arm, bent low and scooped Dominic from Seth's arms with the other hand. The baby's tears faded almost as suddenly as they'd started. Then Travis stood, cradling both brother and sister in his arms, bent his head low over theirs and hugged them both for a long moment, prayers of thanksgiving slipping quietly from his lips.

And Jess realized she had no idea who Travis was anymore.

Seth stood slowly and ran his hands down his jeans.

Travis glanced up over the children's heads, from her to Seth. "Are you both positive my i-d-e-n-t-i-t-y hasn't been c-o-m-p-r-o-m-i-s-e-d?" he asked.

"Absolutely," Seth said. "I give you my word."

Willow wriggled in Travis's arms and, without being asked, he set her down.

"Seth is my new friend," Willow told Travis, seriously. "He likes books, too. He has a sister work friend who talks in his ear."

A sister work friend? Yeah, that would do. Her small off-the-grid witness protection team definitely felt like an ad hoc family.

Willow looked up at Jess, her little brows knit. Then she pointed past her and Jess followed her gaze to a colorful painting of a woman. It was the same woman as the one with long, flowing, blond hair she'd seen sketches of in the kitchen. Even with her face turned away from them, the figure was unmistakable.

The little girl asked what Jess was thinking, "Is that you?"

Travis felt heat rise to his face and the fact that Jess wasn't meeting his gaze made it even worse. What could he say? He'd been a broken man when he'd moved to Kilpatrick, having lost something he couldn't tell anyone about. It had felt like a death. Only, the one he'd lost was himself.

When after too many nights of not sleeping, he'd then fallen asleep at the wheel and crashed his tree into a car, the children's dad, Geoff, had suggested he join an art therapy group. Travis hadn't even known what to draw to represent the aching hole inside him. Somehow in the lines his fingers had sketched across the empty sheets of paper and painted on the canvasses had turned into Jess, again and again, even though he'd never once sketched her face or anything that would identify her, let alone told anyone her name or who she was.

"My name is Jess," she told Willow, saving him from

having to come up with an answer. She crouched down until she was eye level with the girl. "I'm your uncle Travis's friend, and I'm Seth's sister work friend."

"I'm Willow." The little girl stuck out her hand and Jess shook it. "Dominic's my brother. He's a baby."

"Nice to meet you, too, Dominic," Jess said. She reached for Dominic's tiny hand and pretended to lightly shake it, as well.

"Clearly we have a lot to discuss," Seth said. There was a mildly amused tone to his voice Travis couldn't quite place. "I want to go over your entire security system, for the bookstore, your apartment and the house where Patricia and the kids live, as well as whatever your internal baby monitor video system has recorded. Everything for the past months."

"It doesn't actually record more than twenty-four hours," Travis said, feeling almost foolish as he did so. "And Patricia's farmhouse doesn't have any security."

He wasn't even sure she had a front door lock that worked, considering he'd never seen anyone in Kilpatrick lock their doors the whole time he'd lived there. And while Kilpatrick had a district police chief, Gordon Peters, he and Travis had definitely gotten off on the wrong foot, thanks to Travis's minor car accident. The cop had made no secret of the fact he wasn't Travis's biggest fan and wasn't sure Travis was responsible enough to be a volunteer firefighter. Probably hadn't helped much that whoever had created Travis's new identity police file for witness protection had given him more than a few fake traffic tickets and citations. Not that Travis himself hadn't racked up just as many in his real life.

Travis closed his eyes for a moment and prayed. *God, I'm thinking too much like a Kilpatrick resident right now and not a cop. Help me get my head back into the game, without losing my sanity in the process.*

He opened his eyes and turned to Seth.

"Obviously, we can all agree I need to keep my c-o-v-e-r," he said, reminding himself that while a lot would go over Willow's head, there were certain words he didn't want her repeating to anyone. "My top priority right now is taking care of these kids and waiting on word about their grandmother. Also, I really need to head downstairs, as there are probably a dozen people inside the bookstore and no one working the counter."

Not that he expected anyone was about to steal anything. It wasn't that kind of town. When Cleo Mitchell had come home from college with her foul-mouthed, abusive ex, Braden Garrett, the whole town had practically risen like a wave to repel him and let him know that his kind of behavior wouldn't be tolerated. When Cleo had asked Patricia for help, the elderly woman hadn't just called both the police and Travis, she'd also pulled her hunting rifle on Braden and told him she'd shoot if he ever came around pestering the poor girl again. Knowing Patricia, the gun might've even had bullets in it.

"Considering your skills, I imagine you know your way around a phone camera," Travis added and Seth chuckled. "If you don't mind doubling as our c-r-i-m-e s-c-e-n-e photographer, that would be awesome, as well as gathering whatever you can from the limited camera systems. Not to mention, I'm sure you know how to track online purchases. Every part of the guy's getup looked like something you could easily buy online. Maybe we'll be fortunate and you'll happen upon someone who bought a mask, jumpsuit, tactical flashlight, work gloves and an electronic voice distorter online and had them all shipped here."

Seth nodded. "On it."

"Great," Travis said. "You can use my laptop to access the security camera and baby video monitor footage. It's clean as a whistle, I have nothing to hide and the password is Tatlow3."

Travis felt Willow's hands on his leg. He looked down into the little girl's huge green eyes.

"The bad man is not a const'uction man, Uncle Travis," she said. "He's the Shiny Man."

Her eyes were so serious, Travis felt the weight of her trust weighing in his chest. She'd gone through so much already. He would not let her down.

"Whoever he is, we'll stop him," he told her, mentally kicking himself for not taking the little girl's fears more seriously earlier. He glanced at Jess and Seth. "Right, guys?"

"Right," Jess said, her eyes locked on Willow's face. "We're really, really good at stuff like this."

Yeah, she was. Better than he'd ever been.

"Now, can you show Seth how to close the playhouse door and take him downstairs?" Travis asked Willow. "I'll meet you downstairs in the kitchen in one minute."

Willow nodded and Travis watched as the little girl walked over to the big hacker and very seriously showed him how to do the three little pink-and-purple flower-shaped latches Travis had built on the outside of the door. Then he stepped back and gestured for Jess to join him.

"I want you to stick with me," Travis said. "If that's okay with you? I want someone to have a second pair of eyes on these kids."

"Absolutely." She nodded then her arms crossed. "Are other people going to be asking if I'm the woman from the pictures? I saw the sketches in your kitchen, too. Also, your file didn't mention anything about you having children in your life."

He wasn't sure which one was going to be easier to explain, so he started with the first.

"People in this town think she's my ex-fiancée," he said. "I've never confirmed the gossip or told anyone her name, but rumor is I moved here when she left me at the altar. It's…it's very hard to have any kind of secrets in a town where everybody knows everyone else's business."

And he'd never done anything to dissuade the rumors or to shoot them down. It was as good a reason as any as to why he walked around like a man whose world had ended. He'd needed a cover story and the town's rumor mill had created one for him.

Yet, as he watched, shock and confusion filled her eyes. Then her lips twitched slightly and, for a second, he almost thought she was going to laugh.

"You have no idea how devastated I was when I

moved here," Travis said. "I felt like I'd died or that someone I loved had. I was depressed and snapped at everyone. I stopped eating, sleeping at night or showering. I practically lived on coffee. I was basically the worst version of me you'd known dialed up to a hundred. I even fell asleep at the wheel and hit a tree.

"But Willow and Dominic's parents were there for me. They dragged me out to church, board game parties and Bible study with them. Patricia made sure I ate. I needed to come up with something to explain what I'd lost. This mystery woman and the rumors people constructed around how I'd lost her, became like a metaphor for that."

The hint of a smile dropped from her lips. She wouldn't understand. How could she when he couldn't even begin to understand it himself? Yet, as her eyes held his for a long moment, he felt something tighten in his chest.

"Come on! Let's go!" Willow's voice tugged his attention away from Jess. Willow was now leading Seth down the stairs, back toward the main floor, holding his hand tightly, and something in Seth's bewildered gaze left Travis with the sneaking suspicion the hacker had never held a child's hand before.

Yeah, he remembered that feeling all too well. It hadn't been that long ago.

"I want to show him my paintings," Willow called.

"Okay, but then Uncle Seth's got to go do another job and we've got to close the store and go home for supper," Travis said.

Willow nodded and disappeared down the stairs and

Travis was thankful that her skill at finding new friends had temporarily distracted her from the Shiny Man or the fact that her nan was with the doctor.

"She likes people and people like her," Jess said, only something about the way she'd said it made it sound like a cop observing a target.

He bristled. "You make it sound like that's a suspicious thing."

"No, it's an interesting thing," Jess said. "Because if the Shiny Man was outside her window, that means there's someone in this town who's willing to scare her to get what they want."

Whatever that was. He paused a second, shifted Dominic higher in his arms and started toward the stairs.

"You had a duty to inform witness protection that you lived with children," Jess said.

Even though he'd ignored her earlier comment about the kids, she clearly hadn't forgotten it.

"I don't live with them," Travis said. He started down the steps and she followed. "They live with their grandmother at her farmhouse."

"Don't play games," she said. "Not with me. You've got a playpen in your office, a second playpen in your living room and both a high chair and a booster seat in your kitchen. You know full well you're supposed to report any significant relationships including minor children."

"Need I remind you that my original witness protection officer is dead—" Travis felt his voice sharpen "—after conspiring with criminals at Christmas to steal and sell witness protection identities. So forgive me if I haven't been in a hurry to return the calls of the next witness protection officer who got my case, especially since all he seems to want to do is convince me to leave this town and this life, and start again somewhere new. Judging by your voice mail, you were apparently so suspicious of the broader RCMP that you and some colleagues created your own little task force that's been scrambling to pick up the pieces ever since the auction. Right?"

Jess stopped partway down the steps. He turned and looked back. She was almost at his eye level and her lips were pressed together tightly, like she was holding words back to keep from saying them.

"Right," she said. "Within minutes of the theft, three colleagues, Seth and I met together, in secret, and formed an elite off-the-grid team to stop the criminals, despite the fact they started trying to kill us almost immediately. But we not only stopped the auction of witness protection files, we've been working around the clock to locate, protect and resettle every single witness whose identity was compromised. Scoff all you want about the RCMP witness protection program after what happened, but my team and I are very good at what we do."

He hadn't exactly been scoffing. But she was talking so quickly now, she wasn't about to let him point that out.

"What people don't know, is that when those secret identities went up for auction on the dark web, hundreds of criminals showed up online to bid on them, leaving some of our worst enemies vulnerable and exposed."

Fire flashed in the depths of her eyes, like flint striking against stone. "Because the moment those criminals slipped out of the shadows and showed up online to bid, Seth was able to extract their data and gather a treasure trove of information about them. It's the kind of vital intel that you and I could've done so much good with back in the day and I wasn't about to let it slip through our fingers. We could use someone with experience dealing with nasty criminal organizations. So I went to bat for the one person I knew had the skills and ability to take these people on and win—you."

His heart stopped. He might've guessed she was calling about more than her message had implied, especially as she'd showed up in person. But was she actually offering him a job to work with her on her team? "I thought you just wanted my advice on a case."

"Not advice, a partner." Her arms crossed. "Specifically, I wanted my old partner back. And not a case. The case. The case that ruined your career and got you stuck here in Kilpatrick. Thanks to the secret identities auction, I found the Chimera.

"He's back in the country and reopening a new operation this summer on the West Coast. It's under the front of a holiday complex and timed for when school lets out. Summer is a prime hunting time for a criminal like that who presses vulnerable people into illegal work. I'm going in undercover as a hostess. This time, I'm going to be the one who locks eyes on him and identifies the man behind the alias, once and for all. And when I do, I won't miss my shot."

THREE

For a moment, Travis stood there. Frozen. Feeling the past he'd given up on and his present world colliding into an uncomfortable tsunami of emotions deep inside his chest. Jess had a lead on the very criminal Travis had let slip away. She was going to risk her life to positively identify the man. And she'd come all this way to ask for his help.

Dominic nestled deeper against his chest. The little boy burbled something that sounded like words quietly to himself and Travis suspected he wondered why they were still standing in the darkened staircase, in between two floors. Dominic had always loved bright lights and movement, especially the paper butterflies Willow and Travis had made for the ceiling fans and Willow's picture book. But it was as if Travis's feet were rooted in place.

"You found the Chimera?" he repeated.

"I did." Uncrossing her arms, she ran her hand through her hair. "Which wasn't easy to do, because when we took down their main operation, he disappeared overseas. But the dark web auction of the witness protection files back at Christmas was so valuable that criminals took risks they wouldn't have normally taken. If it wasn't for Seth, it probably would've all disappeared without law enforcement ever accessing any of it.

"From what we can tell, the main source of the Chimera's power rests in the fact no one has ever made a positive identification of who he even is. Once someone manages to positively identify the man behind the alias and issue a warrant for his arrest, his days will be numbered."

True enough. Complete and utter secrecy had been the Chimera's main source of power. No one knew if he was a wealthy businessman, politician, member of law enforcement or celebrity.

But knowing Jess, she wouldn't just identify him and get out. She'd take him down if she could.

"Two days ago, Seth matched indicators in the IP address the Chimera used in the auction to a brand-new and highly exclusive nightclub opening later this month on the West Coast," she went on. "We created a false identity for me, and I applied for a job. I fly out there in seventy-two hours."

Three days. His heart stopped. He had less than three days before Jess walked into the lair of the most heinous criminal he'd ever investigated.

"Obviously more time would've been ideal from our end to get the operation put in place," she said. "But I'm just thankful they gave us almost a week. Seth created my fake identity based on intel you and I had gathered

in our old case files, so barring any major unseen ca-
tastrophe, it should hold long enough to get me in the
door."

But would she ever make it back out again?

"You can't be serious," Travis said. "If the Chimera
discovers you're a cop, he'll kill you."

"And the Shiny Man might've killed you," she said.
"Whether it's a big international threat like the Chimera
or a small local one like the Shiny Man, we take them
down. This is what we do."

What she did. What he used to do.

He ran his hand over his head, before setting it back
around Dominic's body. The little boy was growing
heavy in his arms. He'd recently figured out how to
crawl and wouldn't want to be carried around much
longer.

"What were you thinking?" he asked. "That'd I'd
wrap up my entire life in Kilpatrick in three days and
join in on this operation?"

"Behind the scenes," she said. "Like Seth. Who, may
I remind you, is also in witness protection and who
we've done a crackerjack job of keeping safe."

His head shook. He couldn't. There was absolutely
no way. And yet, now that he knew what she was doing,
how could he let her risk her life alone, to infiltrate
a vicious gang to take down the criminals who'd targeted him?

"It's a suicide mission," Travis said. "They'll take
one look at you and see an easy mark. You'll be like a
bunny rabbit walking into a wolves' den."

"Well, that's the point, isn't it?" she asked. "It's why

I've got to be the one to go in undercover and take them on. They'll never suspect I'm a detective, I know the organization better than anyone, except maybe you. Plus, they took you away from me."

How was he even being tempted by this? The day he'd entered witness protection he'd never imagined he'd ever want to be anyone other than who he was. But that was before he'd met God, kicked his bad habits, found peace and made friends. There was no way he could turn his back on Patricia and the kids.

"Now that I'm here, seeing all this, I realize how foolish it was of me to ask for your help," Jess said. "Obviously, I made a big mistake coming here. Notwithstanding the fact you're facing your own bizarre Shiny Man criminal that I fully intend to help you catch and see arrested before I leave town. But honestly, I really missed you, Travis. Like, a lot. And maybe I got overly enthusiastic about the idea of working with you again."

An odd lump formed in his throat. "I missed you, too."

Only he hadn't missed working with her. He'd just missed her.

And now, as he stood in a narrow staircase between the second and third floor of the building that had been his home for the past five years, still with someone else's baby in his arms, staring into the beautiful eyes of the woman he'd never been able to forget, he couldn't believe how foolish he'd been to ever let himself imagine a life with her.

"Well, I thought this was just a run-of-the-mill fake-identity, witness-protection situation for you," Jess said, "and that you'd jump at the chance to be back in the game." Her slender shoulders rose and fell. "Clearly, I was wrong."

She moved pass him and kept walking down the stairs.

For a moment the urge to reach for her welled up inside him. Instead he pressed back against the wall, let her pass him and then followed her down the stairs.

"Don't get me wrong…" he said, finding himself talking to the back of her head, just as he'd sketched her with his back to him in picture after picture. "Part of me really wants to. I really liked working with you and it means a lot that you thought of me. Four years ago, I'd have jumped at the offer. Maybe even two years ago, I don't know. But the town of Kilpatrick is my life now. Patricia's become like the mother I never had. And these kids…" His voice trailed off.

She'd reached the bottom of the stairs and he followed her out into the hallway.

How could he explain what it had been like to hear Willow say her first word or to watch Dominic roll over for the first time?

"Like I said, the Tatlows were really there for me," he tried to explain. "Somehow they roped me into family meals and babysitting Willow almost from the get-go. Ever since Amber and Geoff died, I've been doing my best to help Patricia raise them. Watching the kids, making meals, picking them up and dropping them off from school and daycare, whatever she needed."

Jess stopped and turned back. She slowly ran a hand

over Dominic's soft head, her fingertips lightly brushing Travis's as she did so.

"You do realize being in their lives might put them in danger one day," Jess said. It wasn't a question. "Your cover could still get blown. Or the RCMP could insist you move. And how can anyone really have a relationship with you in this town when nobody knows who you really are?"

His phone rang in his pocket. Immediately, Jess reached out her hands for Dominic. He placed the little boy into her arms and pulled out his phone. Caller ID told him it was Willow's kindergarten teacher, Alvin. "I have to take this."

"Understood," Jess said. "I'll join Seth and Willow and give you a minute."

She turned toward the kitchen, tossing her hair around her shoulders just enough for him to catch a glimpse of the hidden earpiece she used to communicate with Seth. In the past, he'd rarely seen her with her hair down, and usually just in those fleeting moments when she'd let her ponytail out before tying it back up again into a tighter one. He'd never been quite sure if she was more attractive with her hair up or down. But one thing was clear. She was even more beautiful now than she'd been in his memory.

Equally focused and determined, though.

"Your instincts are really solid," she added. "I'm sure you'll crack this Shiny Man thing in no time."

She disappeared into the kitchen and the door swung shut behind her.

"Hello?" There was a pause. He could hear the sound of sirens down the line.

"Travis? Hi, it's Patricia." The elderly woman's voice was faint. Her words were slow. "Alvin's letting me use his phone. I'm with him and Cleo in the ambulance. They're taking me to the hospital in Sudbury."

Sudbury? The major city had a much bigger hospital than the clinic in Kilpatrick or even the closest small hospital. But it was also an hour away.

"I'm here," he said, not knowing what else to say. "Willow and Dominic are with me, and they're great. An old friend and her—" *Colleague? Friend?* "—brother are visiting from out of town and they're helping me keep an eye on the kids."

There was another pause. This one was longer than the one before and he suspected it was taking her a lot of effort to talk.

"It's okay," he said softly. "You focus on resting. I've got the kids and they're safe."

"I have a tumor in my brain," Patricia said, and the words seemed to suck all the oxygen from his lungs. "The doctors have known about it for weeks but said at my age it might be safer to just leave it alone than biopsy or remove it. But now, because of the fall, I've been warned that when I get to the hospital they'll be reevaluating things and if things don't look good, they might be sending me straight into surgery."

"Oh, Patricia, I'm so sorry," he said, again his words felt beyond inadequate. He didn't know what outcome to pray for. "You're incredibly strong. We'll all be praying, and if anyone can get through this, it's you."

The kitchen door swung open as Willow shot around the corner and ran for him. She wrapped both of her arms around his leg. He held up a finger to tell her to be quiet. Willow clasped her hand over her lips and nodded seriously.

"The paramedics warned me to make any important calls now," Patricia said. "Just in case I can't make them later. I want you to promise me that if anything happens to me, you'll adopt Willow and Dominic."

Jess, Dominic still in her arms, rushed out into the hallway after Willow, mouthing that she was sorry. Travis looked from the little boy with a cheeky grin to the little girl down by his feet. An ache spread through his chest. Of course, he couldn't adopt the children. He was living under a fake identity. Travis Stone didn't exist.

"Listen to me," he said. "You're going to be fine."

"Don't talk nonsense," Patricia said. "We both know nobody can promise that. I already told my lawyer my wishes and it's in my will. I was waiting for the right time to ask you, but you're always so hard on yourself. My son and daughter-in-law are gone. The children need a family and you're the only family they have left."

Silently, Jess coaxed Willow away from Travis with a smile and a crooked finger. Moments later they disappeared through his study, taking more than one piece of his heart along with them.

"I don't want to go into surgery with this on my heart," Patricia said. "I need to hear you promise me you'll take care of my grandbabies."

Travis closed his eyes.

Help me, Lord, I can't adopt them. But I can't let them go, either.

"I promise I'll take care of them."

* * *

It took Jess less than five minutes of looking to find the orange reflective construction worker's jumpsuit stuffed behind a trash can in the alley at the bottom of the fire escape. With gloved hands, Jess slid it into an evidence bag, not that she expected they'd be able to pull anything from it, considering the rain and the fact Shiny Man had been wearing both a mask and gloves.

She walked back up the fire escape ladder to where she'd left Seth on the second floor. Travis's face had been serious when he'd finished the call, collected the children and gone downstairs to the bookstore. Although she'd told Travis that she'd be right behind him and join him in a moment once she gave Seth a quick hand, Seth didn't exactly need her help. If she was honest with herself, the real reason she'd first told Travis to go ahead without her was to grab a quick breath away from that odd awkwardness she'd felt moving through the air between her and Travis.

Of all the unexpected things that had hit her since she'd arrived in Kilpatrick, that inexplicable and unspoken tension between them was somehow the most surprising. And somehow the hardest to get her head around.

"So, let me get this straight," Seth called as she reached the study window. "We're now dealing with two criminals. A very, very big one called the Chimera, who went on the run to Europe after you and Travis took down his major organization, and a small-time 'Shiny Man' of Kilpatrick, Ontario, who startles people with flashlights?"

"Looks like it," Jess said. She tossed the jumpsuit through the window and then climbed in after it.

"With no connection between them?" Seth asked.

"None that I can see," she said. "Beyond the fact they both chose the end of June to enact their plots."

She suspected Chimera had good reason for that: he ran an entertainment-based cover business. Did the Shiny Man?

Seth shook his head. "You don't think it's weird that we came here to get Travis's help on investigating the really big bad guy he's hiding from, and instead we're now trying to track down some little bad guy in an orange jumpsuit with a flashlight?" he asked.

"No, I don't," Jess said. "Maybe the qualities that drew Travis to becoming close to Patricia and her family are the same ones that lead them to being victims of the break-in. Maybe something Travis did after moving here, in witness protection, led him to being a target of this Shiny Man. I don't know. I've seen investigations into one criminal spawn into all sorts of other unexpected side investigations, just because criminal circles tend to overlap. In my line of work there are no 'big bad guys' and 'small bad guys.' There are just criminals and it's my job to stop them all."

Whether they trafficked dozens of people like the Chimera or terrified one amazing little five-year-old girl. She paused and looked around Travis's study. The room definitely had all the usual signs of a struggle, including what looked like the contents of Travis's desk scattered across the floor. But judging by the number of books that had been knocked off the shelves, the Shiny

Man had also been looking for something. She picked up a small antique handgun off the floor. Even with the barrel welded shut, she imagined it was still worth a hundred dollars. Not to mention Travis's laptop hadn't been touched and there was probably sixty dollars in cash still in the remains of a broken glass jar.

"Travis said he was late picking the kids up," she said. "Maybe our Shiny Man hadn't been expecting to find anyone here."

"Except he definitely went after Patricia," Seth said. He held up a small tablet computer. "Watch this."

The video was black and white, and both the quality and angle were terrible, but she could see clearly enough that Patricia had been standing on a rolling ladder when the masked Shiny Man had slipped through the back door, slowly crept up on her and pulled a weapon like something from a horror movie.

"He's got a gun trained on her," Seth pointed out, "and it looks like he's going to shoot, or threaten her at gunpoint, but instead his flashy light goes off and he drops the gun. When the light stops flashing, Patricia's on the ground, he's got the gun back and is running up the stairs to Travis's apartment."

Where Willow and Dominic were. Jess's chest tightened as it dawned on her just how much worse the situation could've been.

"None of this makes sense to me," Seth said, setting the tablet down on the desk. "Why pull a gun only to accidentally drop it?"

"Because he's an amateur, he's nervous, or both," Jess said. "Doesn't make him any less dangerous, though."

"Well, I don't know how long we're going to be here," Seth said, "but I'm upgrading the entire security system in this apartment, the bookstore and Patricia's house before we leave. Because this whole lack of a system they've got here is painful." He shook his head. "This is why I couldn't be a cop."

"Because you don't like doing legwork?" she asked.

He laughed. "No, because I don't like problems I can't solve. Travis is in witness protection because the Chimera put a bounty on his head. Even if I had missed some online chatter about Travis's identity being uncovered—which, believe me, I didn't—anyone working for someone like the Chimera would either take him out with an instant shot or kidnap him for questioning. Instead, his place is tossed by a total amateur."

An amateur in a rather effective disguise, who'd been wearing gloves.

"Actually, it's not the slightest bit unusual for someone who's been the victim of one type of crime to be targeted by completely different criminals," she said. "People look for soft targets."

"Did you see the size of Travis's biceps?" Seth snorted. "Believe it or not, I was a high school athlete once before I became a computer chair doughboy, and I know how much work and time it takes to build up that much muscle. Nobody could say Travis is soft."

True. But physical weakness wasn't the only type of vulnerability. And the fact the Shiny Man was an amateur didn't make him any less dangerous.

"I'd better get downstairs," she said. "He's going to want to take the kids home."

"Did you figure out your cover story?" Seth asked.

"I'm an old friend." She turned toward the door. "And you're my brother-friend-colleague. But we'll go with 'brother' for short."

"And did you figure out why he has sketches of you up around the apartment?" Seth called after her.

"Apparently the back of my head is a dead ringer for that of the imaginary woman who left him at the altar," she said.

Seth was chuckling about that as she walked into the hallway. She hit the bottom of the stairs, followed the sound of chatter down the hallway and came out into a somehow both large yet cozy bookstore.

It felt like over a dozen pairs of eyes turned to look at her at once, of every demographic from children to the elderly. Three men in volunteer firefighter uniforms stood by the coffee counter. A group of teenagers and young parents sat around a colorful carpet on which Dominic and several other babies were playing. A man with a trim white beard and a green Harris's Bakery apron was talking to an older woman with long dark braids by a shelf of thrillers.

For a moment her eyes alighted on the uniformed cop by the door and, to her surprise, he met her gaze. He was in his early fifties, she guessed, with the build of a man who still hit the gym, dark hair that was graying at the temples and eyes that seemed to scowl despite the neutral line of his mouth. A warning shiver brushed her spine. Who was that?

"There you are," Travis called. He crossed the floor to her, his arm outstretched.

"Yup, here I am." Her smile felt oddly wobbly, but she figured that might be good for her cover.

A wide and lazy grin crossed Travis's face, but she could tell it was tight at the corners and more than a little uncomfortable. He reached her side and lightly touched his hand against the small of her back, sending a gentle warmth through her core.

"Everyone, this is my friend Jess." He turned toward the room. How many people in this town had heard the rumors about his fictional ex-fiancée? How many would wonder if it was her? "I'm sure she's looking forward to meeting everyone, but she and her brother drove a long way to get here today, it's been an exhausting day, and she arrived to the chaos of Patricia's accident. I've got to take Willow and Dominic home. So, I've got to kick you all out and lock up. But I promise, I'll call the community phone tree the moment I hear anything about Patricia."

She glanced to his face and met his eyes, and for the first time could see the depth of worry floating there. He knew something—something that was bothering him a whole lot, but which he wasn't yet ready to tell her. For a moment Jess stood there, waiting for some clue to what her next line should be, when Willow made a beeline for her across the room and launched herself into Jess's arms even before Jess realized she'd opened her arms to catch her.

"Where's Seth?" Willow asked.

"He's still upstairs, but you'll be seeing him later," Jess said.

"I told the police about the Shiny Man," Willow said. "And I told them there'd been an intruder in my apartment and we'd scared him off," Travis added. "You don't need to make a statement, if you don't want to."

"Actually, I want to," Jess said. She pulled away from Travis, took Willow's hand and strode across the room toward the uniformed cop, feeling Willow skip as she walked beside her. "Excuse me, Officer?"

A polite smile crossed his lips as a neutral and far more professional look filled his eyes. So apparently he knew well enough to hide the previous flicker of hostility.

"Can I help you?" he asked.

"I'm Travis's friend, Jess Amie." She reached out her right hand to shake his, keeping her left looped through Willow's.

"Nice to meet you." He took her hand and shook it briefly. "Gordon Peters, district chief."

"I hear Travis and Willow told you about the intruder—" she said.

"It wasn't an int'uder," Willow interrupted loudly. "It was the Shiny Man!"

Something flickered briefly in Chief Peters's eyes. Like he'd been tempted to roll them and caught himself. Okay, so clearly he didn't believe her.

"Well, I need to confess that I pulled a gun on him," Jess said.

The cop's eyebrows rose. But it was nothing compared to the sound of Travis's sharp intake of breath behind her. She reached into her pocket, pulled out the antique weapon from Travis's study and held it up.

"It looked like he and Travis were fighting," she said, "and I guess it was instinct."

And I'm not saying this was the gun I pulled. I'm just holding it up.

She dropped the weapon into the officer's hand. He turned it over and glanced at the welded muzzle. Then he handed it back.

"I think I have all the information I need," he said. "If you think of anything else significant or spot this orange-clad man, call the police immediately." Chief Peters turned to go then paused. "And please tell Patricia, I hope she feels better soon."

Twenty minutes later Jess was sitting in Travis's red pickup truck as he drove down Main Street and out of town, while Seth trailed behind them in her car. The sun was setting, turning gray clouds dark blue, as she sat in the front passenger seat, with Willow and Dominic in the back. She couldn't help but notice that car seats for both kids were already in the truck and that when he plugged his phone in, it automatically opened to a playlist of children's tunes. He turned on the music and set it to play out of the back seat speakers. Then he waited until Willow was distracted by singing to Dominic before saying anything more than small talk.

"That was a cute trick with the g-u-n," he said, keeping his voice low and a watchful eye on the kids in the rearview mirror. "What was the point?"

"Because the intruder knew I pulled a g-u-n," she said. "I don't know if the S-h-i-n-y M-a-n was someone in that room or how fast rumors spread in this town, but I didn't want them thinking I was hiding anything."

He nodded thoughtfully. "Smart."

She resisted the temptation to point out she was good

at her job. Especially since she wasn't quite sure why she was feeling defensive.

A blue sign told them they were leaving Kilpatrick and invited them to come back soon. The smattering of buildings faded behind them. For a few minutes they drove through trees, then turned off the rural road onto a narrower unpaved road. Travis slowed the vehicle to a crawl and took one more glance at the rearview mirror.

"My landlady might be going into surgery," he said, raising the back seat music even louder and lowering his voice even more to ensure they wouldn't be overheard. "She has a brain tumor and the fall might've aggravated it. Someone will call when they know something. But in the meantime, I'm going to be awake and watching my phone."

"I'm so sorry," she whispered.

"Thanks," he said.

The truck slowed and the trees parted. A two-story farmhouse lay ahead. A wide wooden porch swing rocked gently on the long front porch.

"Is Willow's room on the second floor?" she asked.

Travis nodded as he parked the truck. "The kids share a room. It's around the side."

Seth pulled in behind them, turned off the engine and hopped out of her car.

"I can't leave the kids," Travis said before opening his door. "They need me. I'll do what I can to help you prep for your mission against the Chimera and I'd appreciate your help in turn figuring out who the Shiny Man is. Won't be the first time we've worked two cases at once. But I'm not going anywhere and I'm not leaving Kilpatrick."

Something firm and protective rumbled in his voice. "Got it," Jess said.

Travis plastered a grin on his face and got the kids out of the vehicle in turn, promising them he'd make spaghetti for dinner. They all started toward the house and motion sensor lights clicked on to greet them. But still, Travis's tone of voice and the look on his face twisted something inside her chest.

As much as he might need and even appreciate her help, Travis didn't want her there.

Her footsteps stopped as they reached the porch.

"I'm going to join you guys in a minute," she said. "I need to make a quick phone call to my and Seth's friend Liam."

RCMP detective Liam Bearsmith was steady, level-headed, and the longest serving RCMP officer on her and Seth's team. He'd seen it all and survived to shrug it off. In her experience, he was the perfect person to talk to when she was rattled.

"Sounds good," Travis nodded. "Cell phone reception is better outside the house."

Seth's eyebrows rose. "You want me to join you, Jess?"

"No, I'm good," she said.

Seth's sense of humor was always good for lightening the mood. But right now she needed something other than that. She waited as they went inside and closed the door. Then she pulled out her phone, opened the Contacts file and found Liam's number. Her thumb hovered over it. Then she paused and walked around the side of the house.

Lord, I need Your guidance. I feel really confused

right now. I felt like I was meant to come here, but apparently not for the reasons I thought. Help me know what I'm doing here and what I'm supposed to do.

The motion sensor lights switched off, plunging the world into darkness before she'd barely taken ten steps. She walked further away from the house and pressed Liam's number. Thick trees pressed up against the narrow dirt laneway on both sides.

"Liam Bearsmith," His stern and professional voice was there in an instant.

"Hey, Liam, it's Jess," she said, even though she knew he had Call Display. "I'm guessing Seth filled you in."

"He did," Liam said. "I heard you left Travis at the altar."

Was it her imagination or did a hint of laughter move through his voice?

"Don't believe everything you hear."

The movement to her right was so sudden she barely had time to try to reach for the gun at her ankle before she felt a sweet-smelling rag clamped down hard over her face. There was a fleeting glimpse of the shiny orange sleeves of a construction jumpsuit. Then her head was yanked back hard and the barrel of a gun pressed into the side of her head.

"Drop the phone." The voice behind her was menacing, male and distorted like he was speaking through a voice box. "You and I are going somewhere quiet to talk."

FOUR

Jess would know the sickly sweet smell of chloroform anywhere. But this was the first time she'd felt a rag soaked in it pressed up against her face, filling her lungs and threatening to pull her under. Instinctively she turned her face to the side, creating a tiny bit of distance between her nose and the rag. She forced her brain to overcome her fear, and focus. Chloroform wasn't instantaneous, she could still breathe and it felt like her attacker's dosing of the rag was light. For now, her biggest worry was the gun. Her fingers ached for her own concealed weapon. *Help me Lord!* If only she could reach her gun.

"I said, drop the phone!" The Shiny Man's distorted voice rose.

She let it fall from her hand, praying that Liam would hear what was happening and alert Seth and Travis that she was in danger. The only question was whether they'd reach her in time. She thrashed from side to side, gasping for non-drugged air wherever she could.

The Shiny Man lifted her up and she felt her feet

leave the ground as he tried to drag her backward. She bit his wrist so hard he shouted in pain and dropped her. She hit the ground and barely managed to tuck herself into a roll, as her body tumbled on the rough forest floor. Already she could feel the chloroform coursing through her. How long until she passed out? She didn't know. Only that her body felt heavy and sluggish. She was growing weaker. But she wouldn't give up without a fight.

She forced herself to her feet. But her fingers felt thick and unsteady as she reached for her ankle holster, fumbling in vain as she struggled to remove her weapon. The drowsiness in her head grew heavier. *Help me, Lord! I can't get my gun out!* She gritted her teeth. If she managed to pull it, would she be steady enough to make a shot? If they wrestled for the gun, would she kill him or herself? She forced a deep breath into her lungs and reminded herself that if he wanted her dead, he'd have killed her already.

The Shiny Man charged at her.

"Stop!" she called. "I have a gun!"

The figure hesitated.

"Who are you?" she shouted. "What do you want?"

He didn't answer. Instead, he just loomed over her, an indistinct figure clad in orange-reflective gear with a silver buglike respirator mask covering his face. He looked more like a creature than a man.

Her head swam. Drowsiness beat over her like a wave. Panicked prayers filled her heart. She'd managed to fight through the drug so far. All she had to do was to keep fighting, stay conscious and stop him from taking her long enough for someone to find her. He took an awkward step toward her.

"You want to talk?" she called, hoping the bravado filling her voice would make him doubt the potency of the chloroform. "Come on then! Let's talk!"

"Jess!" Travis's voice floated toward her, faint and distant in the darkness. "Where are you?"

"Travis!" she shouted. "I'm here—"

The blow came hard and fast as the Shiny Man launched himself at her, catching her by the neck and knocking her down onto her back. Her head smacked against the ground. Darkness swam before her eyes.

"Jess!" Travis called. "Jess, where are you?"

She couldn't answer. She could barely even breathe, as the Shiny Man crouched over her, holding her down with a gloved hand at her throat.

"Who are you?" the Shiny Man demanded. His voice distorted, creepy and unnatural thanks to the voice box hidden inside his insect-like mask.

Come on, Jess, stay focused! Underneath it all he was just a man, like every other criminal she and Travis had taken down and put behind bars.

"Who. Are. You?"

"Jess," she croaked. Even drugged, scared and caught off guard, she'd let herself die before she blew her cover.

Travis's voice faded, taking her hope with it. He was running in the wrong direction. The Shiny Man leaned in closer until she could feel the weight of him against her chest.

"What are you doing here?" the Shiny Man asked in his odd, mechanically distorted voice.

She shook her head, like she couldn't speak, and gasped for breath until he loosened his grip on her throat.

"Visiting Travis," she said. She swallowed hard. "We're...we're old friends."

"You're lying," he said.

She blinked. Why would he possibly say that? "I'm not!"

"Then why hasn't he ever mentioned you?"

What? The question sent shivers of fear coursing over her.

It was personal. Whatever was going on, and whatever this man wanted, he knew Travis and considered this personal. Travis had told her it was impossible to keep a secret in a town this small, where everybody knew each other's business. And yet she'd never realized how ominous that could be until now.

"Who are you?" But even as words slipped her lips, she knew he wasn't going to answer.

The sound of Travis's voice disappeared. The Shiny Man leaned in close. The pressure increased on her throat again as his words came out in a long, electronic drone. "Why. Hasn't. He. Mentioned. You?"

God, please help me get my words right.

"I don't know, but he drew pictures of me!"

The Shiny Man recoiled. She gasped, as just as suddenly the intense pressure left her windpipe.

"He painted and drew pictures of me," she said, "in his art therapy group. They're up in his apartment. He didn't tell anyone my name, but people in town knew we were engaged. I think I broke his heart."

She felt ridiculous saying it, blurting out details of some fake romance between her and Travis. But it was the only way to protect Travis's identity or her cover.

He swung back, his hand raised, and she'd barely had time to throw her arm up in defense before the light struck her. This time it was a strobe, flickering on and off in a sudden barrage of light. Then he struck, shoving the chloroformed rag back over her face, harder and stronger this time, until it threatened to suffocate the breath from her lungs.

Help me, Lord, I'm going to pass out!

"Jess!" Travis's voice rose again in the distance.

The Shiny Man grabbed her by the throat and yanked her up.

"Give Travis a message for me." The Shiny Man's voice grew into a high-pitched whine like something out of a nightmare. "Tell no one about this. Don't do anything out of the ordinary or change your daily schedule. Don't talk to police. Don't talk to anyone. Otherwise, I will take the children, and then I'll come kill you."

The Shiny Man tossed her backward. Darkness swept over her.

"Jess!" Travis called. "Shout if you can hear me!"

But he was too far away. She wasn't going to make it.

Travis shouted her name into the darkness, prayers filling his heart as he pushed his body through the trees. "Where are you?"

Moments ago he'd seen a strobe light, disorienting him and flashing somewhere in the trees. Now the night was dark around him.

Lord, please help me find her.

"Jess!" He called out to her in the silence and pressed on.

How had he let her just go out alone like that?

He hadn't thought for one moment it would be a problem. He hadn't thought at all. Despite everything that had happened in the past few hours, he still wasn't thinking of the world around him as a potential threat or danger zone. Kilpatrick still felt like home and his own backyard. It was like he'd been caught between two ways of thinking, without fully rooting his mind in either.

And that had shattered the moment Seth's phone had buzzed. He'd looked up at Travis from across the kitchen where he'd been slathering on butter for garlic bread, and told him, "Jess might be in trouble."

Travis tapped the earpiece that Seth had pushed into his hand as he'd rushed for the door. "Seth? Tell me the kids are safe."

"They're absolutely fantastic." Seth's voice crackled in his ear. "Also, the doors are still locked and there hasn't been so much as a rustle in the bushes outside. I'm guessing you haven't found her yet?"

"No." Travis stopped running. "But I will."

He held his breath and listened in the darkness as his eyes finally adjusted to the light now that the large flash had faded. As determined as he was to never go back to the man he'd once been, the former detective inside him was exactly who Jess needed now.

Then he heard it—a faint rustling somewhere in the trees ahead of him and on his left. He ran toward the noise, praying with every step. Then the trees parted and he saw them.

The Shiny Man was dragging Jess's limp body backward through the trees.

"Let her go!" Travis commanded. "Now!"

The figure in orange dropped her body and raised his hand, barely giving Travis time to shield his eyes with his arms as the blinding light flashed around them. When his vision cleared and the light abated, the Shiny Man was gone and Jess was lying alone on the ground. A vehicle engine roared to life beyond the trees.

Travis knelt on the ground beside her, gently brushed the hair from Jess's face and his heart swelled to feel her warm breath against his hand. His fingertips touched her neck. Her pulse was strong.

"Jess," he said softly. "Can you hear me?"

Her eyelids fluttered. "Travis?"

His name left her lips barely above a whisper and a prayer of thanksgiving exploded like fireworks in his chest. "Are you okay?"

"Mmm-hmm." She nodded faintly.

"Are you hurt?" he asked.

"No." She shook her head slightly. "Just sore."

An unexpected smile curled on his lips. Of course she was sore. She was probably aching, bruised and scraped. But she'd always been one of the toughest people he knew.

"I'm…dizzy," she added. "He used chloroform."

His heart stopped. "He drugged you."

"He tried to," she said. "But it's already wearing off…" she said slowly. "He wasn't very good at it… Not enough on the rag… Didn't hold it down long enough… You know, like we learned on the Pembroke case, chloroform is hard to do right…"

Travis chuckled despite himself. Even limp and dizzy, she was all cop. A very good and professional cop at that. Knowing her, no doubt her brain would start spinning a million miles a minute as soon as she fully woke up.

"Well, let's be thankful he didn't know what he was doing, then," he said. He glanced around at the empty night. The sound of the vehicle he'd heard had now disappeared completely. "I'm going to pick you up and carry you, okay?"

She nodded against his hand. He bent down, scooped her up and held her to his chest.

Travis jogged back to the house, holding her as steady as he could. He tapped his earpiece. "Seth," he said. "I've got her."

A sigh of relief filled his ear. "She okay?" Seth asked.

"Yeah." Thankfully. But his own chest was still aching from the way his heart had been pounding.

"Kids are still great," Seth said quickly, and gamely, and Travis suspected he was putting on a cheerful voice for them. "Pasta's done and drained. Apparently, Willow wants 'shaky cheese'?"

"Grated Parmesan," Travis said. "Top shelf of the fridge. Two shakes." His pace slowed as he saw the lights of the farmhouse between the trees. "Stay cool and don't freak out, but Jess has been chloroformed. Not enough to pass out completely, but enough to make her dizzy."

Seth emitted an odd strangled noise, like he'd been about to exclaim something but then caught himself.

"Been there," Seth said. "Not fun."

Had he now? Travis vaguely remembered Jess saying Seth had been in witness protection, but he'd been so focused on his own situation, Patricia and the kids, he'd barely asked her about her team, if at all.

"I'm going to keep her away from the kids until she's woken up and recovered." Travis said. "Can you grab me a couple of juice boxes from the fridge and leave them on the front porch?"

"Will do," Seth said. "Also, I hope you don't mind, but I accessed Patricia's security system on my phone. Took me two seconds to hack her password. It's a single-camera system that only covers about five feet from the front door, but at least she has one. I'd like to upgrade both her home and bookstore to something a lot more secure before Jess and I leave."

"Thank you," Travis said. He needed help, whether or not he wanted it. He could only sit there with his metaphorical wheels spinning in the mud for so long, before accepting a push. "Thank you for everything, actually. I'm sorry if I seemed irritated or ungrateful with you guys earlier."

"Pfft, don't worry about it," Seth said and Travis could hear the grin in his voice. "I irritate people all the time."

Travis used to, too. He looked down at the woman in his arms. As grateful as he was that Jess hadn't forgotten him, he still cringed to know just how crabby and short-tempered he'd been back when they'd worked together. That job had been like a shoe that didn't fit properly and so had pinched with every step. Whatever he was made to do, it hadn't been that.

He broke through the trees, with Jess in his arms. The front door opened. Seth waved in silent greeting, set two juice boxes down on the porch and closed the door again. The motion sensor lights flicked on as he crossed the lawn, bathing the world in pale yellow light. He looked down at the woman in his arms, as light and shadows moved across her face. He realized she hadn't argued that he should put her down and let her walk. That worried him.

She opened her eyes and looked up at him. "I feel like there's something important I need to tell you but my memory is foggy."

"Give it a moment, your mind will clear and it will come back to you," he said. "You've been drugged and you're probably in shock."

"Also thirsty," she said. "I need water."

"Already on it," he said. "Actually, I got Seth to bring us juice boxes, figuring the added sugar would help with the shock."

She smiled. "You're thinking like a cop."

"A volunteer firefighter actually," he said. "I'm much better at that than I was as a cop."

Her forehead wrinkled. "Because you'd rather fight fires than people?"

Because he was better at saving people than spending weeks getting inside the minds of criminals. Just because he could get his head around how evil people thought, didn't mean it was good for him.

"The job's mostly basic paramedic stuff, search-and-rescue, and public safety," he said. "We almost never fight actual fires."

He reached the house, walked up the steps and stopped at the wooden porch swing. It was still too early in the season for Patricia to set the pillows out on it yet. Her husband had built it for her when they'd gotten married. Willow and Dominic's mother, Amber, had been sitting on it when their father, Geoff, had proposed. And now, it was where he sat with Jess.

He shifted her onto the seat beside him. She leaned against his shoulder, but thankfully she stayed upright. For a long moment he just sat there, the swing rocking slightly beneath them, until the motion sensor lights switched off again and he had to wave his hands over his head to get them back on. Then he glanced down at Jess. "How are you feeling now?"

"Thirsty and dizzy," she said, "with a very foggy brain, but okay." Her words were still slow and heavy, but her voice was definitely stronger and clearer.

He reached for a juice box, careful not to jostle her, balanced it between his knees, and slipped the straw loose of its plastic sleeve and popped it through the hole. Then he handed it to her. Her fingertips brushed his as she took it from him. Then she took a long sip.

"That was impressive," she said. "You're really good at that."

"What, opening juice boxes?" he asked. "Yeah, I've had a lot of practice. The hardest part is getting the straw out of the plastic sleeve without dropping it."

He waited while she took another longer sip and then

winced slightly and glanced at the box. The liquid was purple, the contents probably less than five percent actual juice and the flavor was confusingly named "apple berry." But Willow loved them.

"So, drawing, painting and juice boxes," she said. "Also, I've noticed you've put on quite a bit more muscle. Any other new talents you've developed?"

"A few," he said. "I play first base on the local baseball team. I can build and start a fire without a lighter or matches. I can break plastic zip ties, if I can get my arms at the right angle. I tried my hand at pottery and made a few almost-symmetrical mugs. My big plan for this summer is to take the kids to the lake and finally learn how to skip stones. I watched a lot of online tutorial videos and took a lot of hobby classes when I moved here. I was pretty bored."

"Anything you can't do?" she asked.

"Math," he said. "I'm still terrible at anything math related, and I can't spell."

She chuckled slightly and drained the juice box. He reached for the next one and this time she did her own straw.

"You were right," he added. "I was a good cop. A very good cop. But it wasn't good for me."

She pushed off his shoulder and sat straighter. Then she crossed her legs and pressed her back into the seat.

"I was on the phone with my colleague Liam Bearsmith when the guy jumped me," she said. "He snuck up on me from behind. I'm really embarrassed that I didn't manage to grab my gun. But it was in my ankle holster and he picked me up."

"And he drugged you," Travis added, fighting the urge to rub her shoulder. Instead he set his hands on his knees.

"Still." She frowned. "I hate having to be rescued. Even by you. If it had been on my waist, I'd have gotten to it sooner. If I wasn't so little and short, he wouldn't have been able to pick me up. And if I'd been paying more attention, he wouldn't have been able to get the jump on me—"

He cut her off. "And if raindrops were doughnuts, we'd all eat like kings."

He'd forgotten this about her. How she'd ramble, dither and doubt herself, until he cut her off, got blunt and helped her refocus. How someone so amazing could double-guess herself was beyond him.

She blinked. "That's not how the expression goes."

"It is around here," he said. "There's also one about bacon growing on trees. Now, what else can you remember?"

"He was in full Shiny Man garb," she said, "including the creepy insectlike respirator mask and voice box. I bit him pretty hard, right in between his glove and sleeve, so he should still have a mark on his wrist from that. He said he wanted to question me. Not kidnap me or kill me. He wanted to take me somewhere to ask me questions…"

"What kinds of questions?" Travis asked.

"He wanted to know who I was…" She straightened as if something had suddenly clicked behind her eyes. "He wanted to know why you'd never mentioned me. I told him that I was an old friend and he called me a liar."

Travis felt like cold water had suddenly dropped from above, drenching him through to the skin. The Shiny Man knew him. He was from Kilpatrick. He was one of them. *Help us, Lord.* "What did you say?"

"I told him I was the nameless, mystery, ex-fiancée woman you kept drawing," she said. "It was an established part of your existing world."

And not completely untrue.

"He also told me to give you a message," she said. "Do nothing. Don't go to the police. Don't do anything out of the usual, or he'd come after me and the kids."

Considering the fact District Police Chief Gordon Peters seemed to have a pretty low opinion of Travis, and had no idea who Travis and Jess really were, Travis wasn't even sure he trusted the man enough to risk letting him in and getting him involved. Something tightened in his chest and he took a long, deep breath in and out, trying to loosen it.

"Good news is, this is more evidence he's not working for the Chimera," she said, "and that the Chimera and the Shiny Man are two completely unrelated cases. The Chimera only uses highly trained and deadly mercenaries from Eastern Europe. The Shiny Man is definitely an amateur, not a pro. His chloroform technique was lousy, and he hasn't been all that great with a gun."

And that was supposed to make him feel any better?

"Patricia is in surgery because of the fall," he said, hearing his voice bristle. "He was trying to abduct you. This is no minor thing."

"I didn't say it was minor!" she said. "I didn't even imply it. But surely it's good news that this means your cover hasn't been blown and Shiny Man isn't working for an international criminal but someone you know. You can figure out who he is, we can have him arrested and move on."

"This is my home." Travis's voice rose. "These people are my family. I know you don't get it and think of all this as some fake little life I've been playing at. But this is who I am now. You said, like two minutes ago, that you hated having to be rescued. Even by me. Do you think I like having to be rescued by you?"

"Don't change the subject." A puzzled frown filled her eyes. "That has nothing to do with this. And you don't get it. You're a big, strong guy who's never had to worry about someone picking them up like a rag doll."

"And you've never blown your cover," he said. "Or been shaking so bad with a blinding headache from caffeine withdrawal that you missed a shot. Face it, Jess, you came to Kilpatrick on a rescue mission." He hadn't meant to raise his voice but still it seemed to echo though the stillness of the night. "You came to rescue me. Whether you intended it that way or not. I'm in witness protection because my cover was blown. And in two days you're going in undercover to clean up my mess and take down the criminal I let get away."

"Nobody blames you for that—"

"I blame me!" Travis said.

"And I came to ask for your help." She reached for him. Her hands grabbed his and held them tight. "Because I need you."

Her eyes locked on his and he could see their blue depths searching his. And suddenly he felt an odd feeling filling up inside him. He wanted to sweep her back into his arms. He wanted to hold her, to protect her from danger and never let her go.

"No, you don't need me," he said and yet somehow his hands stayed locked in hers. "I keep trying to tell you, but you're not hearing me. I was a wreck back when we worked together. I was depressed. I was irritable. I barely slept and chased caffeine shots down with coffee to stay awake."

"You were still the best partner I ever had," she said, "and I was at my best with you, Travis. I don't know why all this is happening, but maybe we were brought back together for a reason, so I could help you stop the Shiny Man and you could help me stop the Chimera."

His phone buzzed in his pocket. He pulled his hands away from hers and checked it. It was Alvin, the kindergarten teacher. He answered. "Travis speaking."

"Hey, Travis," the younger man's voice was hesitant. "Cleo and I are on our way back to Kilpatrick now. A doctor will be calling you soon with an update, but I wanted you to hear it from us first. Patricia's in a coma."

FIVE

Two minutes later, Travis stood in the kitchen doorway, feeling the blood drain from his legs as the doctor confirmed what the kindergarten teacher had told him. Complications in Patricia's surgery had caused swelling in her brain, so they'd put her in a medically induced coma until the swelling went down. Now there was nothing to do but wait and pray.

He watched through the doorway as Jess helped Seth pass out garlic bread and scoop up pasta for dinner. The happy scene was such an anathema to everything the doctor was telling him. If Patricia died, he already knew the police might rule it an accidental homicide; there was more than enough reason for that in the footage Seth had taken. But in his heart, Travis would always know the truth—it was murder.

He closed his eyes and prayed. *God, I know that You and I haven't known each other as long as we should have, but Patricia and her family got me through so much. Please, heal her, and help me stop her attacker and be the protector her grandchildren need.*

His hands were shaking as he thanked the doctor and hung up the phone. Patricia was the heart of Kilpatrick. How could anyone hurt her? And what for? He walked back into the kitchen in a haze and focused on putting a smile on his face, scooped himself some pasta from the stove, sloshed some sauce over it and took his usual seat at the table.

He noticed that Jess had found the jar of fresh baby food he'd thawed in a bowl of warm water for Dominic and was slowly feeding it to him with one of his plastic baby spoons. Travis resisted the urge to ask her if she'd checked the temperature first, and instead relied on the fact that Dominic was gurgling happily and eagerly eating to reassure him that Jess had probably done okay.

Jess glanced up and met his eyes, and he could see questions floating there. Back when they'd worked together, it had felt like they'd been so close they could read each other's minds. And after all this time, it was amazing how her eyes, in a glance, could still pull him in.

"Are Jess and Seth coming to the school concert t'morrow?" Willow asked. Her chin rose. "I'm playing the tr'angle!"

The word *no* crossed his mind, but he stopped it from passing his lips. How could he let her go up on stage in a school concert tomorrow knowing the Shiny Man was on the loose? And yet, the man was clearly an amateur and a coward. It's not like he'd make an attempt on Willow's life in front of the entire community or that he'd even made any attempt to come after the child.

"We'll see," Travis said.

If he was honest, he had no idea what tomorrow held. He appreciated Seth's offer to update the security systems, but his brain couldn't process much beyond that. Especially with the news of Patricia's condition so fresh in his mind. If it was up to him, he'd take the children and leave town. But he didn't have legal custody. And despite being like a mother to him, Patricia didn't even know who he really was, let alone that he was a former cop like the son and daughter-in-law she'd lost.

Willow's lips pursed like she was pondering something serious and Travis found himself bracing for her next question.

"Seth use' too much shaky cheese," Willow said seriously.

Jess laughed and raised an eyebrow at Seth. "Did he now?"

"Yes!" Willow nodded vigorously. "I tol' him he's only allowed two shakes! He took three!" She held up three fingers to illustrate.

"And I told her that in Seth's kitchen, Seth's allowed as many shakes of Parmesan as he wants," the hacker said, grinning. "Especially on popcorn."

"Seth puts a lot of cheese on his popcorn," Jess admitted. She leaned toward Willow conspiratorially. "Then he gets it all over his computer."

Willow giggled. Jess straightened and turned back to Seth.

"Seth needs to remember that everybody's family is different," Jess said with both a gentle smile on her lips and a firmness to her tone. "It's important to respect the way other families do things and, right now, we're in Willow and Dominic's home."

Travis felt a smile curving on his lips. He watched as she slipped another spoonful of food into Dominic's mouth, wiped off the overflow that dribbled from his grinning mouth and then deftly slipped a forkful of her own pasta into her own mouth without breaking stride. He wondered if she'd ever wanted to have kids of her own. Or if she, like him, had worried a career as an undercover detective, and the specific type of exhausting and emotionally challenging police work they did, would make it hard to be there for a family.

"This is Nan's house, too," Willow said.

"It is," Jess said. "It's Nan's house, too. Will you show me around after dinner? I'd love to see your special storybook."

Willow smiled and nodded. "The cover is on u'side down!" Then she frowned. Her lip quivered. "I wish Nan was home."

Travis felt something like pain stab his heart. He'd already fielded a few uncomfortable questions about when Patricia was coming home and was sure he'd be facing more as bedtime grew closer. *Help me, Lord. The hardest weight I've ever had to bear was being strong for Willow, Dominic and Patricia through everything they've lost. Help me be the strength they need right now.*

"We can pray for Nan if you want," Jess said. "Maybe at bedtime?"

"Can we pray right now?" Willow's chin shook.

"Absolutely," Jess said. She set the cutlery down. "We can all pray for Nan right now."

The lump in Travis's throat grew tighter. He saw Jess glance his way, not asking his permission but still double-checking that he was on board, and for a moment all he could do was nod.

Willow reached across the table and took Travis's hand on one side and Seth's on the other. The hacker blinked as if lost and Travis found himself feeling a ping of sympathy for him. Yeah, he remembered how weird his first unexpected Tatlow family prayer circle had been, too.

Jess gently held Dominic's tiny hand in hers and gestured to Seth to do likewise. Then Jess reached for Travis's hand and he felt Jess's fingers slide between his.

Willow's prayer was short and sweet, with all the earnestness of a five-year-old, partly asking God to heal her Nan and partly some the familiar words she knew from the usual prayers he knew she said at night at bedtime. Then she said "Amen" very loudly and firmly. Everyone followed suit, hands were dropped and he felt Jess slowly pull her hand from his.

Moments later Seth excused himself from the table to make a phone call. Willow asked to be excused and Dominic started fussing. Jess pulled Dominic from his high chair and bounced him on one hip while she cleared the table. Travis joined her at the counter and scraped off the dishes into the compost bin that Patricia kept under the sink. She glanced back over her shoulder and watched as Willow disappeared into the other room.

"Guessing it wasn't good news from the hospital?"

Jess said, bending her head close to Travis's and keeping her voice low.

"No, it wasn't," he said. "But I thought I was doing a pretty good job of hiding it."

"Oh, you were," Jess said. She turned to face him and something inside him startled to realize how quickly he'd gotten used to having her there. "But a former partner knows things, especially after working over fifty cases together."

Yeah, he guessed some connections never went away.

"You're not broadcasting it," she added. Her voice faltered, like she wasn't quite sure what to say. "I mean, you're not making it obvious."

"Like I used to?" Travis asked. "It's okay. We can both admit I used to let things get to me and was pretty open about broadcasting my feelings. But that's the good thing about kids. You can't be in a miserable mood without them being puzzled and hurt by it. Loving them helped me learn a lot about growing up and parking my own feelings long enough to help someone else."

He stretched out his hands for Dominic. She eased him into his arms.

"I'm guessing we'll talk after the kids are asleep," he said, "and strategize what we're going to do about both the Shiny Man and the Chimera." He couldn't remember the last time he and Jess had tried to strategize solutions for two unconnected criminal investigations at once, let alone ones that were so very different. "I'm guessing you're going to want to call in your team. And I'm sorry if I seemed dismissive about them earlier, but I admit we need the help. I need your help."

"Sounds good," she said, and he was thankful she seemed willing to let his earlier rudeness go. Then again, Jess had always been too forgiving, at least when it came to him.

"Bedtime will take about an hour," he added. "And since you've told Willow you'd like to see her story-book, you're part of it now. First we've got teeth brushing and face washing, then pajamas, then stories, then bedtime songs and finally prayers. It's an hour-long operation."

Jess's nose crinkled in a look he knew all too well. It was the one she got when she was pondering something that didn't make sense. Only in this case, the thing that didn't make sense was him.

"What?" he asked.

"You pray," she said. "You didn't used to pray."

In fact, he used to make fun of her for praying, despite the fact he'd found the sound of it comforting.

"Is this something you do for Willow?" she asked. "Or part of your cover?"

"It's something I do because that's who I am now," he said. "It's something Patricia, Amber and Geoff encouraged me to do. When they saw how jittery I was, and how I relied on caffeine and was constantly stressed out, they encouraged me to join this recovering addicts group at their church. It was alcoholics mostly, but also one woman who was addicted to pills and a couple of men with gambling problems."

He took a deep breath and let it out slowly.

"Honestly, my addiction had been to my job, not the caffeine," he admitted. "But the emphasis on prayer really helped. I needed someone who knew who I was—who I really was, my entire past and everything I'd been through. Even if I couldn't be fully myself with anyone else, God knew me when no one else did, and that helped."

Jess nodded, and far more understanding than he deserved hovered in the blue depths of her eyes. She had no idea how absolutely beautiful she was in his eyes, inside and out. Just like she'd never know how tempted he'd been to start up a romantic relationship with her and how thankful he remained that he never had.

"I'm not the man I used to be, Jess," he said. "I'm better now. It took a lot of hard work. Work that I'm very thankful for, I might add. I know I fought coming here and going into witness protection with everything I had. But it made me a man I actually like being and that means everything to me."

He turned to walk out of the kitchen. Then he stopped, took a deep breath and mustered his courage for what he needed to say.

"And I'm sorry." His eyes locked on hers in the old farmhouse kitchen that felt like a second home. "Because no matter how you remember us, I know for a fact that you deserved a far better partner and friend than me."

He said the words kindly, but still they hit her like the slap of a cold wave striking her face. He turned and walked out of the room while she stood there, not even knowing or understanding why his words had struck her the way they had.

There was a rhythmic knock on the door. She looked up. Seth was leaning against the door frame.

"Crazy day, huh?" the hacker said.

"Has it only been a day?" she asked.

"Actually, it hasn't even been half a day," Seth noted. "You know, I never thought I liked kids. And maybe I still don't. I mean two aren't exactly that big a sample size. But, wow, I do like those two."

"Yeah, so do I," Jess said. "They're pretty amazing."

And it was clear that they adored Travis just as much as he loved them, which made everything even more difficult and complicated than it already was.

"I went ahead, called the hotel and canceled our rooms," Seth went on. "Travis invited us to bunk here and I figure you wouldn't want to leave him and the kids." His shoulders rose and fell. "And I'm way too curious about this whole mess to leave without finding out how it all ends."

She felt a weak smile cross her lips. "Thanks. We'll have a team meeting once the kids are asleep. Call in Liam. Maybe Noah."

The fifth member of their team, Mack Gray, was on some well-deserved time off helping his social worker fiancée, Iris, rebuild her life after leaving witness protection.

"Yay, we're getting the band back together." One eyebrow rose. "Are you okay, though? You look like something rattled you."

Jess sighed, turned back to the sink and pressed her hands against the edge of the counter.

"Travis just apologized to me for not being a better

person back in the day," she admitted. The nice thing about Seth being the kind of guy who just randomly blurted out what he was thinking was that it gave her the leeway to do the same. "He said he was sorry he wasn't a better partner and a better friend, because I'd deserved far better than him. I'm not even sure what he means by that, and it makes no sense, because he was the best guy I knew."

Which Seth, out of everyone, knew, considering how much she'd blathered on about Travis on the drive up.

"Okay, so maybe Travis was the best man you'd ever known and worked with," Seth said. "But that doesn't mean he's wrong."

She blinked. "I don't get what you're saying."

"Are you sure you don't?" Seth asked. He paused a moment as if waiting for her to admit something, but she wasn't sure what. Then he shrugged. "Look, I'm not proud to admit this, but I've had a pretty rocky ride through life so far. I was a bully and jerk in high school. I always had technical know-how, but instead of using it to get a Ph.D., build something awesome and change the world, I became a hacker—a criminal hacker—who tried to stop really bad guys by breaking the law. Then our friend Noah saved my life. Literally pulled me out of the trunk of a car and got me through a hail of bullets."

He blew out a hard breath.

"I ended up in witness protection," he went on, "then the huge data hack happened, you all landed on my front door and invited me to join your team. That was the first time I even started believing I could be one of the good guys and use my skills to be part of something… Which is probably the most I've ever told you about myself, despite the fact we've been working together since Christmas."

It was, which made it all the worse to admit she still didn't get his point.

"I appreciate you trusting me enough to tell me that, but…" she started.

"But you don't get why I told you?" Seth asked. "It's like this. I had teachers telling me to join the police or military when I was sixteen. But I didn't believe I belonged with the good guys. In fact, when I thought I was going to die in that criminal's trunk, part of me believed I didn't deserve to be rescued."

He looked down at the floor for a moment and ran his hand across the back of his head.

"People can be really bad at knowing what they deserve," Seth said. "Some think they deserve way too much and others think they deserve too little. I believe you when you say Travis was the best guy you knew and the best cop you ever worked with. In fact, I think you had a major crush on him. Maybe you still do. But I also believe him when he said he wasn't the best guy back then and you deserved better. Both things can be true at once and, like I said, I read his file." He turned and headed back into the living room, throwing one more sentence at her back over his shoulder as he went. "Those kids are definitely special, though."

The hacker disappeared through the doorway before Jess could say anything more or even think up a response. Seth was wrong. Travis had been an excellent detective. Sure, he'd been temperamental and grouchy sometimes, especially when he hadn't eaten or slept. And yes, she'd always found him attractive, in a whole host of ways from his lazy smile, to his chocolate-brown eyes, to his wry sense of humor, to the blunt way he talked that helped her mind focus, to the way he threw himself into his work.

She hadn't had a crush on him. Or, if she had, it didn't mean that was the only reason she'd wanted him to join the team, was it?

Yet, the question still rattled in her head as she went upstairs and joined him in getting the kids ready for bed. She moved through the evening routine, reading stories from Willow's old and faded storybook with its hard cover sewed on upside down, learning the songs and joining in the prayers. She enjoyed every moment and her heart swelled to see how well Travis cared for the kids. But still what Travis and Seth had said, along with her own memories, rattled faintly in the back of her mind. And the more she saw the man he was now, the more she realized just how much happier and calmer he was than the man he'd been.

It was an hour and fifteen minutes before the children were asleep and she and Travis went downstairs to join Seth at the dining room table. Seth's laptop was open in front of them. Liam and Noah sat in two different boxes on the camera screen. She made introductions as they sat.

"Travis, meet detectives Noah Wilder and Liam Bearsmith," she said.

"Nice to meet you," Travis said.

"Likewise," Liam replied.

"Noah and his fiancée, Corporal Holly Asher, were on the front lines when the computer hack of witness protection files happened," she said. "They were the ones who ultimately took the hackers down and stopped the auction."

Out of the corner of her eye, she saw Seth raise his hand, as if wanting to point out he'd had a major role in stopping the auction, too. "With Seth, of course," she added. "Liam is one of the best undercover detectives in the country, especially in terms of organized crime, and has been coordinating the relocation of witnesses whose identities were stolen. Our fifth member, Mack Gray, is taking some well-deserved time off."

"Small team," Travis noted.

"A small team, but the right team," Liam said. His voice was usually serious, but now, for some reason, it was almost stern. "Considering the fact we had every reason to suspect the theft of the witness protection files was facilitated by someone inside the RCMP and that law enforcement had been infiltrated, we decided it was best to keep it tight and off the grid."

"Why you five?" Travis asked.

Jess took a breath and went for brutal honesty. "All four of us detectives were on some form of probation at the time."

"And I was just sitting around bored in witness protection," Seth interjected, "with all my talents sadly wasted."

"It enabled us to work off the grid," Jess continued, "outside the usual chain of command."

"And highly effectively," Liam added firmly.

But in her peripheral vision, she saw Travis's eyes widen. "What kind of probation?"

"I had a family issue holding up my security clearance," Noah offered.

"And I was on medical leave," Liam said. He grimaced as if the memory had left him with a bad taste in his mouth. "Crooked cop blew my cover to some criminals I was targeting, and they weren't too happy. They jumped me, knocked me around a bit and I ended up in a coma. Thankfully, another cop closed the case I was working on and I pulled through with nothing worse than recurring headaches."

Truth was Liam had nearly lost his life, but he brushed it off like it was nothing.

Travis turned to Jess. "You never told me that you'd ever been on probation."

"Well, I was." She said the words directly and without smiling, feeling herself slide back into full detective mode. Seth had all but accused her of letting her personal feelings for Travis cloud her professional judgment. She wasn't about to be accused of being emotional now.

"As you well know, I put up with a lot of harassing comments and sexist remarks during my career, people belittling me and thinking I didn't know my stuff because of how I looked. When I was on undercover assignment last summer, a fellow detective got a bit fresh with me and grabbed me, so I gave him a quick jab to the gut to get him to let me go."

"What happened?" Travis asked.

"I winded him," she said, "and he went down hard."

Seth snorted and a slight smile turned on Noah and Liam's lips, too, and she realized that in all the time they'd worked together, this might've been the first time she'd told the story.

"I didn't hit him that hard. Just four knuckles, not even a punch." She held up her hand, fingers folded over, and tapped her knuckles as if to demonstrate. "No injury. Just left him gasping for breath. But I caught him before he could exhale, so he went down like a sack of potatoes."

Liam barked out a laugh. It was so sudden and unexpected that it sent Seth and Noah chuckling.

Travis's face was serious. His hand brushed hers in a gesture that was both protective and caring. Warmth spread through her body.

"Were you okay?" Travis asked.

"Oh, he was fine—"

"But were you okay?" Travis prompted.

She pulled her hand away. No, she'd been embarrassed.

"Of course." She folded her arms and leaned them on the table. "There was a disciplinary meeting. He claimed he hadn't touched me, but that even if he had, he'd just been swept up in his character. Of course, I claimed it was what I believed my undercover character would do under the circumstances. I chose suspension over mediation."

Because she didn't want to be forced to apologize for demonstrating to a room full of vulnerable people that it was okay for a woman to fight back and defend herself.

"Anyway—" She felt her tone tighten. "This is my team."

And she was proud of them, regardless of what Travis might think.

Travis leaned his elbows forward on the table and, for a moment, didn't say anything. Then he clasped his hands together.

"I'm going to be blunt," Travis said. "Part of me is really touched that Jess thought I could add something of value to your team and your operation against the Chimera. But I have no interest in ever leaving my life in Kilpatrick."

"A life where you violated the terms of your witness protection agreement by expanding your family without notifying the RCMP," Liam pointed out. His smile was tight and somehow more intimidating than a frown would be.

"With all due respect, it's unrealistic to think anyone's going to integrate into a new life in witness protection without forming friendships," Travis said, the tightness of his smile now matching Liam's, and a warning flashed in his eyes. "Patricia Tatlow is my landlady and my friend. Her grandchildren are like family to me. Patricia didn't choose to raise them alone. Her son and daughter-in-law were both cops who died trying to combat drunk driving. I stepped in to help raise their kids. I won't apologize for any of that." He turned to Jess. His eyes met hers. "And now Patricia's in a medically induced coma."

He might've been talking to the entire team, but his

eyes were locked on hers alone. Then he turned back to the group.

"She had an existing brain tumor that the attack by the Shiny Man exacerbated," Travis added. "It's too soon to know if she's going to make it. But before she went into surgery she asked me to adopt her kids if she didn't make it. I agreed to do everything I could to protect them."

Jess felt a gasp slip her lips. She wasn't the only one. But it was Noah who spoke for the group.

"Of course you know you can't adopt children under a false identity," he said gently.

"I do." Travis sat back and crossed his arms. "But I'm not about to let them lose everything and everyone they know and go into foster care."

"My parents were foster parents," Noah said, his voice somehow growing even softer and yet firmer at once. "I grew up with a lot of foster brothers and sisters. I understand that would be far from ideal, but there are a lot of wonderful foster families in the world. Social services might even find someone within their community."

Travis's chest deflated. "No disrespect intended."

Noah nodded. "None taken."

Tension seemed to crackle around the group, like a powder keg waiting for a spark. As for Jess, she now felt like she was the one who'd been winded.

"I have a lot of sympathy for the fact you've built a relationship with those kids," Liam said. "Really, I do. But your life stopped being your own when you entered witness protection. Your life has been threatened. Jess's life has been threatened. The children's only living relative is in a coma. As active witness protection agents with the RCMP, we can't just ignore that. If word gets out to the higher-ups that we just sat on the news of any of this, we could lose our badges."

The detective sighed.

"Again, I'm sympathetic to your situation," Liam added. "Really I am. But we need to relocate you to a new witness identity, as long as there's an active threat targeting you, and you can't take the children. With everything Jess has seen and knows about the children, Patricia and the Shiny Man, if she just ignores it all and goes home, you're basically asking Jess to risk her career for you."

The tension grew tighter until she felt like something in the room was about to snap. She took a long breath. Liam was right. She was risking her career. But how could she just turn her back on Travis?

Lord, this whole situation is a mess. Nothing makes sense and everything is at stake. Please, give me wisdom.

"What if we give it forty-eight hours?" Jess said quickly. Her hands rose instinctively, like she was trying to stop an invisible foe. "Two days. No more. Seth needs to upgrade all of Travis's security systems, both at Patricia's house and the store. I need to assist Travis on the Shiny Man case and hopefully help him catch the guy. And even though Travis isn't going to help me in the Chimera case, I'd still love him to go over the file and consult on it."

She glanced at each of the men in turn. "I know it's

unconventional, but so are we. We make it a quick forty-eight-hour RCMP operation to check in on Travis, help him upgrade his security system and deal with a reported threat. The fact he'll also consult on the Chimera case will help justify the length of time we spend here."

"And I can install things really, really slowly," Seth added.

She shot the hacker a grateful smile.

"We can't have any of you risking blowing your cover," Liam said. "You're running a parallel investigation to local police, not stepping on theirs. If it comes to it, you walk away from the investigation in order to protect your identities."

"Agreed," Jess said.

That wasn't exactly a yes but she already knew which side of the fence her team would land on.

Then she turned to Travis. "It's not ideal, I know," she said. "But we're painted in a corner. A lot can happen in two days. Patricia could wake up and recover. The Shiny Man could be caught."

"Or I could have two days left with Willow and Dominic," Travis said, "before they leave my life forever."

SIX

The conversation seemed to move in a blur around him. He nodded at the right places and then, when the subject shifted off the topic and people started saying goodbye, he felt himself stand and walk out the front door. He wasn't even sure if the conversation had wrapped up or if he'd said anything before leaving. He'd just known he'd had to get out of there before he'd said something he regretted.

He pushed through the front door and out onto the porch. The warm and dark June night surrounded him. School would be out in days and summer was almost here. Velvety darkness pressed in on all sides, filled with nothing but the faint whisper of wind rustling in the trees and the threat of impending rain. His fists clenched. For the first time, in a long time, he wanted to yell at the world.

Are you out there, Shiny Man? The words ripped through his mind in a silent shout. *Are you watching me? Who are you? What do you want? Why are you taking my home, my family and my life from me?*

But the words that blazed through his mind never crossed his lips. Instead he dropped down onto the swing, let his head fall into his hands, and prayed.

I'm trapped, Lord. Everything I could even think to pray of seems impossible to ask.

Desperate. That was how he'd felt when he'd first landed in Kilpatrick, alone in a town where he'd known no one and nothing. That was how he felt now.

He heard the creek of the door behind him and knew Jess was there before she'd even spoken.

He glanced up at her without raising his head. "What do I do?"

"Tomorrow or next week, I don't know," Jess said. "But I can think of one practical thing you can do tonight."

"I'm open to suggestions." It had been a rhetorical question when he'd asked it, but anything beat lying awake worrying. He found himself hoping that she'd cross the porch and sit beside him on the swing again. Instead she crossed her arms and leaned back against the wall.

"I think you should go back to the bookstore and your apartment," she said, "and do a visual sweep of it like you used to. You had this way of pacing a crime scene in the middle of the night and seeing things others had missed."

He looked up. "Because I was an obsessive and stressed-out insomniac who didn't sleep."

"Maybe," she said. "But you were also really good at what you did. Nobody could get inside the mind of a criminal like you could, and that wasn't just the coffee. You know this town. You know who the Shiny Man could be. But the whole time you were in the bookstore after he attacked, you were either taking care of Patricia, the kids or me. You need to go back there as a detective. Even if you don't find anything or see something you didn't see before, it could still jog your memory."

He let out a long breath. She wasn't wrong.

"Just go," she added. "I'll stay here and watch the kids."

"No." Travis stood. "I want you with me. You've always been a great detective, and I'm beyond rusty."

Not that he much liked the idea of leaving the kids. But they were fast asleep and it was a safer option than bringing them along. Thankfully Seth was able to set up a video camera feed from the kids' room, allowing Travis to keep an eye on them.

Rain had already started falling lightly by the time Travis pulled the truck down the long, unpaved driveway and out onto the road. He glanced at Jess in the passenger seat beside him.

"For the record, I know your team isn't wrong," Travis said, "and neither are you. I can't stay somewhere where there's a target on my back, and I can't adopt the kids, become their legal guardian or even take them with me. I just hate it. Okay? I hate what's happened. I hate what could happen and I hate the position it puts you in."

"Nobody blames you for hating it," Jess said softly.

He clenched his jaw and looked straight ahead.

"But you do blame me for not wanting to go back to being an undercover cop though, right?" Travis asked.

"I will go over your entire file on the Chimera and your plan to go undercover. I'll give you any feedback and insight I can, and I'll pray for you all day every day. But I'm not going back to that life."

They kept driving. The world was black outside his windows. Raindrops splattered against the darkened windshield. He glanced down at his cellphone and the video feed of Willow and Dominic sleeping peacefully in their beds. Then Travis's eyes went back to the road ahead.

Lord, I've never loved anything in the way I love these kids. Please, help me protect them.

A car pulled onto the road behind them, low and dark, with only one headlight. It was rare to see another vehicle on the road this late at night and this car was trailing far too close behind them. Travis held his breath and tried in vain to see the figure behind the wheel. The car turned onto a side road and was gone.

"It's just that you seemed to really love your job," Jess said after a long moment. "You were motivated, you were focused, and you always kept me on track. Nobody cared about the work more than you. You brought all this heart into the work and you were amazing at it."

"You're right," Travis said. "I was motivated. I was good at it. And I thought I loved it. But I didn't see how it was killing me inside or what it was doing to me. Maybe it was right for me then, but God wanted to lead me to better. I loved working with you. But I hated myself." His shoulders rose and fell. "Can you forgive me for wanting to rescue just two kids when there're hundreds out there I could be helping to save?"

She startled. "It's not my place to forgive," she said, "and I'm the last person to judge anyone for not wanting to be in this line of work. It's hard." She crossed her arms and leaned back against the seat. "Did I ever tell you I was engaged to be married once?"

"No." Who in their right mind would've ever let a woman like Jess get away?

"It was a very long time ago," Jess said. "I was nineteen. He was a few years older and didn't want me to go into the police academy, because he was in med school and thought it would be too hard on our relationship if we both had big careers. As the wedding got closer, it became clear that he wanted me to be a housewife. He told me I had to choose between him and being a cop."

She took a deep breath and let it out slowly, rolling her shoulders back like she was tossing off a weight. "I told him I loved him, but I felt called to law enforcement. He canceled the wedding."

The buildings of Kilpatrick moved past the window. Pain stabbed at Travis's heart. "I'm so sorry."

She held up a hand, palm forward, as if trying to push back any sympathy he might be feeling.

"It's okay," she said. "He was clearly the wrong person and, if anything, it hardened my resolve to spend my life rescuing as many people from as many bad situations as I could. If I had a family, I'd still be going after criminals like Chimera, I'd just be doing it from a different angle or a different way that didn't have me in the direct line of fire." She blinked and looked out the window. "Why did we pass the bookstore?"

He winced and did a careful U-turn on the empty

small-town street. A shiver ran up his spine as he suddenly realized he'd been so involved in Jess's story that for one fleeting moment he'd forgotten where he was.

Forty minutes later, Jess stood in Travis's study and watched as he paced like a caged animal around the space. The skies had opened in the past few minutes, sending sheets of rain beating against the building. Thunder rumbled in the air punctuated by spikes of lightning that split the night. Tension crackled around the room and seemed to encircle Travis like an invisible force field, and Jess wasn't sure why. He'd been tense in a way she couldn't put her finger on ever since she'd told him the story about her failed engagement. She didn't know why.

"What are you thinking?" she asked.

"That we're not going to be able to get any usable fingerprint or DNA from this chaos," Travis said. He stopped and waved his hands through the air as if drawing an invisible circle around the mess. "The Shiny Man was wearing gloves, a jumpsuit and a respirator mask. It's like he'd spent hours online researching how not to leave evidence."

"Remember the man in Aurora who murdered three women?" Jess asked.

"You mean, Mr. No Evidence?" Travis snorted derisively. "The guy who practically drenched his crime scenes in bleach to destroy DNA? I can still remember the chemical smell. And how he sat there in the interrogation room and smugly tried to tell me that since there was no DNA evidence, I'd never get a conviction." He shook his head. "Like the fact his car and apartment were covered in bleach wasn't suspicious."

If she remembered correctly, it had taken Travis four hours to get a signed confession.

Travis glanced at his cell phone, and she followed his gaze. Willow was curled up in a tiny ball, but Dominic had tossed his blankets off and now lay on his back like a starfish. Both kids were fast asleep.

"So what does your gut tell you about the Shiny Man?" she asked.

"Nothing new," Travis said. He set the phone down on the desk with the screen visible. Thunder roared outside, momentarily drowning out Travis's voice. "He wants something. The fact he trashed my study makes that clear. The fact he challenged Patricia means he might've also had a personal beef with her. The way he questioned you implies he also knows me personally and was surprised by the sudden appearance of a woman in my life he didn't know. His Shiny Man getup implies this wasn't an impulse decision and he put a lot of thought and planning into it."

And he hadn't been counting on Jess.

Thunder crashed again, moments after the last burst and harder than before. The lights went out, plunging the apartment into darkness except for the pale glow on Travis's cellphone. Her hand shot to her weapon as she steeled herself. Then a tiny yellow light flickered on ahead of her in the darkness and she could see Travis's face in the flame of a lighter.

"The power grid's not the best around here," he said.

He bent down and rummaged around on the floor. "Thankfully, I have a few candles."

She watched as Travis moved through the darkness, pulling round candles from the wreckage, lighting them and setting them on the shelf, where they created small pools of light in the darkness.

"We need a list of potential suspects," she said. "Anyone who the Shiny Man could be. Names we can look into. People we can investigate. Who has motive to hurt you, those kids or Patricia? What's up with District Chief Gordon Peters? Why doesn't he like you?"

"I don't honestly know," Travis said. "But we definitely got off on the wrong foot when I dozed off at the wheel and crashed into a tree. He was against my joining the volunteer firefighters and sometimes makes cryptic remarks about running a background check on me. But my witness protection identity should be solid and problem free. The only black marks on my name are some speeding tickets, which is kind of ironic considering I got plenty of those in real life, too. As far as I know, he was never married and had no kids. He always seemed sweet on Patricia."

"Any romantic interest?" she asked.

"Between the district police chief and Patricia?" he asked. "Maybe, but if so, she shot him down."

She made a mental note to ask Seth to take a look into Travis's faked background to see if there was anything else there Chief Peters would have a problem with, as well as running a check on the chief himself. "Have you racked up any other enemies in town? Any animosity among the other firefighters?"

"No," Travis said. She watched as he closed his eyes. "Judging by the security footage that Seth was able to pull, Shiny Man's initial target was Patricia. She's a sixty-eight-year-old female. One marriage, to a cop who died of a heart attack twelve years ago. One child, a son, who died while working a roadside check stop, along with his wife, who was also a cop." His eyes snapped opened. "So, we look into all three of their professional records. Any one of them could've arrested somebody who's held a grudge or has a family member who did. The fact it took them so long to make a move could be because they were behind bars."

Jess felt a smile turn on her lips. "Good start, Detective. Who else? Think motives. Anyone stand to gain financially from her death?"

"Just me." He shrugged. "If she's left me her property in trust for the kids. Although, the baker next door, Harris Mitchell, has tried to pressure her several times to sell the bookstore. He can be a bit pushy and wants the property to expand his business. He threatened to sue her once over a fallen tree that did some damage to his property. But it was really a minor thing."

"And the baker's daughter, Cleo, went with Patricia to the hospital," Jess said. "Any other business dealings?"

"Not that I know of," Travis said. "One woman who has a local candle and incense shop was annoyed Patricia wouldn't stock her stuff. But again, it's petty stuff."

"Anyone in town with a criminal record?" she prompted.

He watched the rain pound against the window for a long moment then he turned back.

"No," he said. "But there used to be. Braden Garrett. He's twenty-four, has a drug problem and multiple arrests for minor things. He used to date Cleo and he was a nasty piece of work to her. She'd run to Patricia for help when his temper got out of control. Once when Patricia heard Braden yelling at Cleo outside the store, she grabbed a shotgun from behind the counter, marched out, pointed it at him and told Braden if he ever threatened Cleo again, she'd shoot him."

Jess whistled. "And why haven't we interviewed him?

"Braden left town almost two years ago," Travis said. "Nobody's heard from him since. I think Cleo's now dating Alvin, the new kindergarten teacher. His fiancée left him recently when she got a great job overseas. Life in a small town is a veritable soap opera."

He glanced back at the cell phone, and his face paled. "The camera's gone dead."

"It's probably just a power outage. Call Seth."

Thunder crashed outside again, dragging her attention back to the window. Lightning flashed for a split second, illuminating the world outside. A gasp rose to Jess's lips.

The Shiny Man was standing on the fire escape, watching them.

SEVEN

The lightning faded, leaving nothing but darkness outside. But still the shape of the Shiny Man's form floated before her eyes like a shadow.

"He's…" She swallowed hard and forced her tongue to find words. "He's outside! Shiny Man is outside on the fire escape."

And she was going to stop him. She felt Travis's hand reach for her arm in a gesture that was both protective and reassuring, but she pushed past him. Already she could hear the sound of footsteps clanking on the fire escape. No, the Shiny Man was not getting away this time.

"Call Seth and check on the kids." She crossed the floor in three strides and shoved the window open. "I'm going after him."

Wind and rain whipped against her face and seeped past her into the room. The fire escape was empty, as were the steps below her. Then she glanced up to see a figure disappearing onto the roof.

"Jess!" Travis shouted behind her. "Wait!"

She didn't even pause to answer. Instead she dove through the window and sprinted up the slippery metal stairs as rain drenched her body and wind buffeted against her.

"It's not safe!" Travis's voice floated faintly behind her.

Of course it wasn't. Any more than it had been safe when Travis had faced down the Chimera or any of the numerous times that either of them had gone up against a criminal. But this was who she was and this is what she did. And she'd never be the woman who stood comfortable, safe and dry in a candlelit room with a handsome man, when there was a criminal out there she had the power to stop. No matter how much she might want to.

Help me, Lord. Help me stop this criminal and end this nightmare for good.

Jess reached the top of the fire escape and paused with her head just below the line of the roof. Silence fell above her, besides the sound of the storm surrounding her. She readied her gun and risked raising her eyes above the edge. At first glance, the roof seemed empty. Then the lightning flashed again, and she saw him. Shiny Man was pelting away from her across the roof. Where did he think he was going?

She sprang after him and pulled her weapon. "Stop!"

Stop! Police! She felt the words cross her lips silently as her brain barely kept her from shouting them. She couldn't blow her cover. Not even to stop him. Shiny Man paused and lingered for a second at the far corner of the roof. Then he leaped, his arms outstretched, the fabric of his jumpsuit flapping around him as he disappeared from view.

No!

A crash sounded from below. Anguish and frustration battled inside her as she ran across the roof, through the pounding water, feeling her footsteps threaten to slip underneath her and send her falling after the criminal.

Jess reached the edge of the roof and looked down. The rain and darkness blocked her view. Then, with a snap, the power came back on and the ground came into view. There was no one and nothing there but a scattered pile of garbage bags and boxes she guessed the criminal had used to break his fall. Yeah, she wasn't about to try to jump down after him.

A sigh left her body. She holstered her weapon and started back across the roof to the fire escape. As she walked down the stairs, she could hear the faint sound of Travis's voice and guessed he was on the phone with Seth. She reached the second floor and glanced through the window. Sure enough Travis was standing in the middle of the study with his phone to his ear. His eyes met hers, and she could see the question there. She shook her head.

He ended the call.

"Fill me in as we drive," Travis said. "Power's out at the house. Kids are fine, but Willow's woken up and I want to be there for her. She's pretty scared of storms."

She climbed through the window and had just reached back to close it when a light switched on in the second floor of the building opposite them. From the apartment above the bakery, Jess assumed. It disappeared just as quickly, plunging the window back into darkness. But not before she'd caught the outline of a woman against the curtains.

"Did you see that?" She turned to Travis. "There was a woman at the window."

He nodded. "I think that was Cleo."

"Do we talk to her today or tomorrow?" she asked.

There was a benefit to both. Conventional wisdom was that witness memories were clearest immediately after something happened, but when working undercover sometimes it made more sense to wait to find the right time to talk to someone.

"Tomorrow," Travis said. "We'll find a way to make it a natural conversation. Knocking on neighbor's doors in the middle of the night is a bit tricky, and whatever reason we come up with is going to become town gossip, especially if I'm going to be waking up Harris."

"Sounds good," Jess said.

She closed and latched the window. They sheltered their heads with jackets as they sprinted to Travis's truck. He pulled the truck onto the road and drove toward the farmhouse.

"The Shiny Man was reckless and desperate," she said. "He just ran across the roof, in a storm, and then leaped off, falling into a pile of garbage. He could've been killed or seriously injured. It's the behavior of the kind of criminal who does not think, does not plan...and might even indicate emotional instability or substance abuse. And that doesn't fit at all into our earlier analysis that his getup implied he put meticulous thought and planning into his crime. So, unless there are somehow two Shiny Men we've got to deal with, we might need to rethink things."

Jess's heart ached as she lay her head back against the passenger seat and looked into the dark and rainy night outside.

Help us, Lord. I have no answers right now, just unanswered questions.

She sensed Travis's body stiffen even before she turned to see the worried expression on his face. His eyes darted from the road again to the rearview mirror. She glanced back over her shoulder. A car with one headlight was trailing them on the empty, unlit road.

"That car was behind us on the way to the bookstore, too," Travis said. "I think we're being followed."

Travis's hands tightened on the steering wheel. He couldn't see the face of the driver behind him in the darkness. But while the world was full of coincidences, he was pretty sure being trailed twice in the middle of the night by a car with the same headlight out wasn't one of them. The vehicle behind was tailgating and inching ever closer. He prayed and sped up slightly. The car behind fell back for a moment, but even before Travis could breathe a sigh, it caught back up with them again, until it was so close that if he risked tapping the brakes it might smash into them.

He glanced at Jess. "I'm going to have to do some fancy driving."

"Go for it," she said.

The trust that shone in her eyes warmed something inside him.

Okay, then. The rain beat down against the truck. The roar was slippery underneath his wheels. A gap loomed in the trees ahead, leading to an unpaved road. He fixed his eyes on it and gritted his teeth, waiting for the last possible moment to yank the steering wheel toward it. The tires spun beneath him. Trees reared in front of the windshield. But he steadied the wheel and the truck flew down the dirt road, branches beating against the vehicle as it jarred and shook along the bumpy ground.

His phone began to ring. He glanced at the screen. It was Seth. He pushed the button to put it on speaker phone. "Sorry, man, I'm kinda busy right now."

"Uncle Travis?" Willow's shaky voice filled the truck. "Will you pray with me? I had a nightmare and the storm's really loud."

Travis felt his face pale as he glanced at Jess. But almost immediately she snatched up the phone, took it off speaker and held it to her ear.

"Hey, Willow, it's Jess. Your uncle Travis is a little busy right now, but I'll pray with you."

Gratitude flooded his heart. Did Jess have any idea how extraordinary she was? Or how thankful he was for her?

The single-headlight vehicle reappeared behind them through the trees. The wipers cut back and forth quickly through the wall of water pouring down over the windshield. He took another sharp turn, the truck swerved again, and they were back on a paved rural road. Thanks to his work in the community, he had a pretty good mental map of the back roads in the area. But with the one-eyed vehicle behind still too close on his tail, he couldn't outrun it forever.

Then a jolt shook through the truck as the car clipped their bumper from behind. The floodlights of a large agricultural supply warehouse loomed ahead. Travis waited until the last possible second, yanked the steering wheel hard and swerved into it. The truck spun in a tight and controlled circle. He hit the brakes, lowered the window and prepared himself to shoot.

"Get down!" he shouted.

The car pulled in after them. Travis raised the weapon out the window and aimed it at the approaching vehicle, praying he wouldn't have to fire. For one fleeting moment, he caught a glimpse of the Shiny Man's reflective jumpsuit and respirator mask in the glow of the complex's floodlights. Then the car swerved hard and its wheels screeched as it pulled back onto the road.

Shiny Man sped off. A prayer of relief and thanksgiving filled Travis's heart. In this battle of chicken, the Shiny Man had lost.

The roads were empty as Travis drove them to the farmhouse through the rain and Jess stayed on the phone with Willow the whole way back. Getting the little girl back to sleep took even longer than it had when he'd first put her to bed. When she was finally settled and asleep, Travis found Jess waiting for him at the bottom of the stairs. The furious sound of Seth tapping on the keyboard came from the dining room.

"Seth's searching online retailers for any Shiny Man–type orders that have been placed for this area," Jess said. "Whoever he is, he didn't buy that respirator mask, tactical flashlight or voice distorter in a town this small. If Seth can locate a recent shipment to the area matching the description of the Shiny Man's gear, he can use that to figure out the address where it was delivered. I've also given him a list of all the potential leads we brainstormed back at your apartment. He'll track them all down and we'll see what he comes up with tomorrow. We'll also talk to Cleo tomorrow, too. For now, I'm going to try to get some sleep. I suggest you do, too."

Yeah, not a bad idea.

"You can take the guest bedroom," he said. "Seth can have the pullout in the study, and I'll take the living room." Not that he expected he was going to be able to sleep.

"Good night, Travis. Let's all pray this all makes a lot more sense tomorrow."

She turned and darted through the door before he could respond, leaving an empty place where she'd been just moments before. Something in his heart tugged after her. Her former fiancé had been wrong. Her passion for her job was one of the best things about her and any man who wanted to take that from her was a fool.

He lay awake for hours, listening to the ticking of the grandfather clock and praying. He wasn't sure when he even fell asleep, but when he next opened his eyes, early morning sun was slipping through the window and across the floor. The sound of cheerful voices filtered in from the kitchen.

He found his phone in the couch cushions—the hos-

Dear Reader,

Your opinions are important to us. So if you'll participate in our fast and free "One Minute" Survey, **YOU** can pick up to four wonderful books that **WE** pay for!

As a leading publisher of women's fiction, we'd love to hear from you. That's why we promise to reward you for completing our survey.

IMPORTANT: Please complete the survey and return it. We'll send your Free Books and Free Mystery Gifts right away. **And we pay for shipping and handling too!** *We pay for EVERYTHING!*

Try **Love Inspired® Romance Larger-Print** books and fall in love with inspirational romances that take you on an uplifting journey of faith, forgiveness and hope.

Try **Love Inspired® Suspense Larger-Print** books where courage and optimism unite in stories of faith and love in the face of danger

Or TRY BOTH!

Thank you again for participating in our "One Minute" Survey. It really takes just a minute (or less) to complete the survey… and your free books and gifts will be well worth it!

Sincerely,

Pam Powers

Pam Powers
for Reader Service

"One Minute" Survey

GET YOUR FREE BOOKS AND FREE GIFTS!

✓ Complete this Survey   ✓ Return this survey

▶ DETACH AND MAIL CARD TODAY! ▶

1 Do you try to find time to read every day?
☐ YES ☐ NO

2 Do you prefer books which reflect Christian values?
☐ YES ☐ NO

3 Do you enjoy having books delivered to your home?
☐ YES ☐ NO

4 Do you find a Larger Print size easier on your eyes?
☐ YES ☐ NO

YES! I have completed the above "One Minute" Survey. Please send me my Free Books and Free Mystery Gifts (worth over $20 retail). I understand that I am under no obligation to buy anything, as explained on the back of this card.

☐ I prefer Love Inspired® Romance Larger Print 122/322 IDL GNTG

☐ I prefer Love Inspired® Suspense Larger Print 107/307 IDL GNTG

☐ I prefer BOTH 122/322 & 107/307 IDL GNTS

FIRST NAME _____ LAST NAME _____

ADDRESS _____

APT.# _____ CITY _____

STATE/PROV. _____ ZIP/POSTAL CODE _____

© 2019 HARLEQUIN ENTERPRISES ULC. "®" and ™ are trademarks owned by Harlequin Enterprises ULC. Printed in the U.S.A.

Offer limited to one per household and not applicable to series that subscriber is currently receiving. **Your Privacy**—The Reader Service is committed to protecting your privacy. Our Privacy Policy is available online at www.ReaderService.com or upon request from the Reader Service. We make a portion of our mailing list available to reputable third parties that offer products we believe may interest you. If you prefer that we not exchange your name with third parties, or if you wish to clarify or modify your communication preferences, please visit us at www.ReaderService.com/consumerschoice or write to us at Reader Service Preference Service, P.O. Box 9062, Buffalo, NY 14240-9062. Include your complete name and address.   LI/SLI-520-OM20

BUSINESS REPLY MAIL
FIRST-CLASS MAIL   PERMIT NO. 717   BUFFALO, NY

POSTAGE WILL BE PAID BY ADDRESSEE

READER SERVICE
PO BOX 1341
BUFFALO NY 14240-8571

NO POSTAGE
NECESSARY
IF MAILED
IN THE
UNITED STATES

◄ If offer card is missing write to: Reader Service, P.O. Box 1341, Buffalo, NY 14240-8531 or visit www.ReaderService.com ►

pital hadn't called. His body ached as he rolled off the couch.

He found Jess and the kids waiting for him in the kitchen. He blinked. The children were dressed, smiling and eating cereal at the table. Jess stood by the counter and held up a kettle as he walked in.

"Good morning," Jess said. "Seth left about twenty minutes ago to go see about updating the security system at the bookstore. I made herbal tea, but I wasn't sure if you still drank it."

"If it's decaffeinated, yeah," he said. "Though I still limit myself to one cup a day, and I no longer drink coffee, pop or energy drinks."

He hesitated a moment, realized there weren't any jobs left to do, so instead slid into a seat beside Dominic's high chair. How Jess had gotten the kids up and snuck them past the couch where he lay sleeping without waking him up felt like some kind of magic trick.

"We have to go to school now," Willow said earnestly. "We're late. It's eight-oh-five."

He let out a long breath. The Shiny Man's instruction to act like nothing was wrong swirled through his mind. Willow's kindergarten and Dominic's preschool were both housed in a well-lit and very secure municipal building and civic center with security cameras, metal detectors and security guards at the door. The lines of sight were amazing and the kids would have dozens of caring eyes on them. It was the safest place for them. And yet, after everything that had happened, how could he ever let them out of his sight?

"What if you and Dominic stayed with me today?" Travis said. "We could have a special day together."

Willow was already shaking her head vigorously. Her lower lip stuck out in a pout. "No. It's school concert day! With all my friends! I'm playing the tr'angle!"

Jess's phone began to ring just as Willow's voice rose to a wail. Jess stepped away from the table and answered the phone.

"Hello? Yeah? Wow... Got it."

She stretched out her hand and offered the phone to Travis. He held up a finger to his lips to ask Willow to be quiet. Thankfully she stopped fussing, although her lower lip stuck out farther than ever.

He held the phone to his ear. "Travis here."

"It's Seth." The hacker's strained voice came down the phone. "I'm at the bookstore. It's been trashed, and I've been arrested."

EIGHT

A small crowd of people had gathered in front of Tat-low's Used Books. Chief Peters had parked his cop car in front of the store and slapped yellow police tape across the door. Travis parked across the street and then slipped Dominic into a solid, reinforced sports-utility infant chest carrier that he pulled from the glove compartment of his truck. Jess noticed it was Travis's size and already set for his broad shoulders. She took Willow by the hand and the four of them approached the bookstore together.

There were at least a dozen people milling around the front of Tatlow's, chattering and gawking, including most of the people she'd seen the night before, like the volunteer firefighters and Harris the baker. She didn't see Cleo, his daughter, anywhere.

As they reached the bookstore, the crowd parted just enough that she could see Seth sitting on the low sill of the huge front window. He was leaning forward, his elbows on his knees, his hands cuffed in front of him.

Chief Peters stood before him, his chest puffed out like an angry robin protecting its yard.

Willow gasped and tried to tug free of Jess's hand to run to him. Instead, Jess scooped her up and held the little girl in her arms.

"Jess!" Willow said. "Tell police Peters that Seth not a crim'nal!"

The little girl's wide eyes felt like a mirror to Jess's own and there was something about the look in them that made Jess's heart swell in her chest. Willow was so bold, so confident, and determined to do what was right. Not to mention incredibly caring. She prayed Willow would never lose those qualities.

"It's okay," Jess said. "Travis will take care of it." She stood back and watched as Travis strode over to Chief Peters.

Travis was in plain clothes, with a gurgling Dominic strapped to his chest, and the chief was in his dark blue-black uniform. But in her eyes, there was no doubting which one carried more authority.

"What is this?" Travis asked. "What's going on here?"

"Travis," the chief said. "There's been a break-in at Patricia's store."

"So I've heard!" Travis waved a hand toward the store. "But that doesn't explain why my friend is sitting there in handcuffs."

Seth's eyebrows flinched. Jess suspected it was only the seriousness of the moment that was keeping him from making some cute comment about the fact that Travis had just called him a friend.

Chief Peters frowned. He had that posture she hated, that of an arrogant man who was convinced he was right. And seeing him step up to a man like Travis, who'd taken down more criminal operations and stopped more vile offenders than Chief Peters could even imagine, galled something inside her. Then a new thought hit her straight between the eyes. The old Travis she'd worked with and known wouldn't have stood for being disrespected. He'd have gotten into Chief Peters's face. He'd have seethed. He'd have let his irritation show. But this Travis, standing there with a baby, was calm, his expression showing nothing more than a polite and clearly exasperated smile.

"Again," Travis said, "why is my buddy in handcuffs?"

"He was walking around inside the store," Chief Peters said. "At the very least, he was aware of an active crime scene and made no attempt to call the police."

"I gave him a key," Travis said.

"I don't think he used a key," Chief Peters said.

"Because the door was already ajar," Seth said, "as somebody else had already broken in." He glanced at Travis. "I quickly ran through to assess what had happened before calling you. For the record, the store's been trashed, but your apartment wasn't broken into."

Because whatever the intruder was looking for wasn't there? Jess wondered.

"Then this guy showed up," Seth said. "I told him I was your friend, but he practically already had one cuff on me before he let me call you."

Travis shook his head. "Come on, you know this isn't necessary. I can vouch for him."

"I ran his file." Chief Peters went for his handcuffs, slowly. "At least someone knows how to stay within the limits and keep himself out of trouble."

Travis wasn't sure what kind of false identity witness protection had created for Seth, but the idea the hacker's file was squeaky clean was funny.

"And I know what's in yours, just so we're clear," the chief added, a bite to his tone. Jess didn't know what he meant, but Travis had said the chief liked to remind him of that. "Rumor has it this guy's sister left you at the altar."

"Well, you know how it is with gossip," Travis said. "Most of it is hogwash."

Jess stepped away and left the men to argue as Chief Peters removed Seth's handcuffs. She had no doubt that Travis was about to win the argument, once the district police chief had done as much posturing as he felt he could get away with. The question was why the tension between the two men existed in the first place. But for whatever reason, Willow definitely didn't need to hear it.

She glanced through the store window. Seth hadn't been joking when he's said it was trashed. It looked like someone had yanked every single book off every shelf, display and surface, until the floor was nothing but a mound of paperbacks. Furniture had been knocked over and even the sweets and coffee counter looked like it had been riffled through. It would take hours to put everything back on the shelves.

Instinctively, she swung Willow around and moved her away from the window. But even as she did so, she knew she was too late.

"Jess." Willow's voice was in her ear in a horrified whisper. "Somebody threw all the books on the floor."

"I know, kiddo," Jess said.

The little girl's eyes grew wide. "Who would do such a thing?"

She shook her head. "I have no idea."

"Books are very special," Willow said. "My teacher tol' me so." Then suddenly Jess felt her try to wriggle from her grasp. "Seth!"

Jess barely had time to set her down before she took off running toward Seth as he ambled handcuff-free toward them. The hacker scooped her up into his arms and hugged her. Jess backed even further away from the crowd and then into the side alley between the bookstore and bakery where hopefully no one could hear them.

"Well, that was fun," Seth said. "I can't believe he actually ran me through the system. Thankfully, whoever at RCMP created my file did a bang-up job and that was even before I enhanced it. Now, here's the interesting part. I got a hit on the address where our s-h-i-n-y friend had his supplies delivered. No owner listed on the property, but it's only about thirty minutes from here."

She thanked God. They actually had a break.

"Don't do spelling!" Willow said sternly. "I don't like it." She frowned. "I need to go to school."

A door slammed at the end of the alley. Jess spun back. The slender form of Cleo Mitchell was walking toward them. The baker's daughter's shoulders were hunched, her arms wrapped protectively around her body.

Jess had worked enough investigations to read the woman in a glance. Cleo was terrified, with that specific type of fear that meant she at least partially blamed herself for whatever frightened her. And while Jess's detective brain knew the young woman was a potential witness to last night's Shiny Man attack, something lurched in Jess's chest to remember what Travis had told her about how Cleo's ex-boyfriend had terrorized her.

Jess smiled warmly and stretched out her hand.

"You're Cleo, right?" she asked. "I saw you getting into the ambulance with Patricia yesterday. I'm Travis's friend, Jess, and this is my brother Seth."

Cleo took her hand awkwardly and, due to the angle of their arms, Jess ended up just squeezing her fingers before dropping her hand.

"I saw you at the store last night, right?" Cleo asked. "My dad said that somebody broke in and trashed the place."

Well, that hadn't been the reason Jess had been there in the middle of the night, but both facts were true. "Yes," Jess said. "Did you see someone on the fire escape last night?"

Cleo nodded. "Did he scare you? Or attack you?"

"He did," Jess admitted. "But I was okay. Why? Did he hurt you, too?"

Cleo's shoulders shook.

"I know who it was," she said softly. "It was my ex-boyfriend. Braden Garrett."

* * *

Moments later Jess stood with Travis, Cleo and the police chief in the alley between the stores while Seth watched the kids a discrete distance away.

"Braden has been trying to get me to talk to him," Cleo said. "He contacted me on all my social media sites, texted me and keeps calling and calling me until I give up and answer."

"What does he want?" Travis asked gently.

Jess noticed the chief's back stiffen slightly. She found herself checking the police chief's wrists for injury but couldn't see them under the uniform.

"Sometimes he tells me he's not a bad guy," Cleo said. "He gets really angry at everyone he thinks wronged him and says that he's going to make them pay. He mentioned Patricia especially, because he's still mad she pulled a gun on him that one time and told him to leave me alone."

Jess met Travis's eyes and watched as his brows rose.

"He misses me and wants me back," Cleo added. "He's says going to come into some money soon. He also said he'd do something really bad if I didn't take him back."

"Like what?" Travis asked.

This time Peters sent Travis a warning glance. And Jess fought the urge to remind Travis it was no longer his job to question witnesses.

"It's okay, Cleo," the police chief said gently before Cleo could answer Travis. "We can talk about this down at the station and I'll get you a Victims Services counselor to talk to if you want. You can file a report against

Braden, we'll put out a warrant for his arrest and we can get a protective order against him."

Otherwise known as a restraining order. While definitely an important tool in protecting people against harassment, somehow Jess doubted this situation was as simple as an old boyfriend stalking an ex. She took a deep breath. The Shiny Man had explicitly told Jess not to go to police. But isn't that what a normal and scared non-cop civilian would do if she discovered another woman was being stalked by the same man who'd frightened her?

"Tell him about the man in the mask we saw on the fire escape last night," Jess blurted.

Chief Peters's eyes spun toward her just like she knew they would. "What man?"

"I saw a man in a construction worker's outfit and mask watching me," Cleo said. "Just standing outside between the bakery and bookstore, like he was stalking me. It had to be Braden. He said he'd been watching me."

"We both saw him on the bookstore fire escape last night," Jess interjected quickly. "He had this really scary mask on that made him look like a bug-man."

"It's a ventilation mask they use in building to protect against fumes," Cleo explained. "Braden used to work construction."

"He startled me when I was walking in the woods last night outside Patricia's home, too, and demanded to know who I was," Jess said. "Guess he figured I was a friend of hers. He ran off when he heard Travis coming. He told me not to tell police."

"Stop." Chief Peters stepped between them and held up his hands. "Not another word about this. You have to stop comparing stories. Otherwise you'll risk muddying each other's statements." He turned to her. "Miss... Jess... I am sorry you went through this, I would be very happy to talk to you down at the station, if you want to file a report and see about getting any help you need. But I have to talk to you and Cleo separately." He glanced at Travis and the look in his eyes grew firmer. "I need to ask you to respect me on that and not try to get involved in this."

Jess watched as something sharpened in Travis's stance. A frown crossed his face and spread to his eyes. Her old partner wanted to dig his heels in and argue. He wanted to question Cleo, and she didn't blame him. Jess slid her hand onto his arm and tugged gently. For a briefest moment, he didn't move, then Travis followed her away from the chief of police and Cleo.

"We're running a parallel investigation," Jess said softly as soon as she was sure they were out of anyone's earshot, "and not interfering with local police. I want to question Cleo, too. But we have to let Chief Peters help her now and it's a good sign he's suggesting a protective order. Meanwhile, Seth has discovered a potential lead on an address outside the city where the Shiny Man could've gotten his equipment delivered. Seth's also having a duplicate of everything the Shiny Man ordered couriered to him."

Travis let out a long breath, but the tension in his body didn't abate any. "I don't know how we're going to figure out what's going on, while still maintaining our covers and protecting the kids."

She knew the feeling. And while the idea that the baker's daughter's ex-boyfriend was stalking those who'd wronged him definitely made a lot of sense, Jess still felt like there were still some major pieces of the puzzle she was missing.

"Our top priority has to be getting the kids away from all this and somewhere safe," she said. "We can't be investigating Shiny Man or hanging around crime scenes with them. Seth's run the schematic on Kilpatrick's civic center and it's as safe a place as we're going to get. What if Seth stays there and watches the kids while we go check out the location?"

She waited a moment while she watched Travis close his eyes and pray.

"I don't like it," he said finally. "But I think it's the best of all the bad ideas."

When they joined Seth and Willow back at the truck, the little girl's anxiety dropped immediately when Travis told her he was taking her and Dominic to school.

Kilpatrick Public School only went up to grade six and was housed in a wing of the city center that also included a library, municipal offices, a recreational center, hockey rink and small auditorium. There were guards on the main door, metal detectors, a buzz-in system that meant everyone entering the building had to check in at the front desk, and a wealth of internal security cameras. Not the kind of place anyone could smuggle a gun or even a flashlight into easily.

Dominic's preschool nursery and Willow's kindergarten classes were part of a large open-concept area attached to an atrium, with benches, tables, chairs and large, leafy plants. Most important, there were huge glass windows that looked into both kids' rooms, so that parents who worked in the building could easily pop by to check on their kids without disrupting class.

Seth positioned himself at a round table that faced both rooms at once, while Travis dropped off the kids. He also confirmed with internal security that no one was to pick up the kids, under any circumstances, but him, Jess or Seth.

"Right," the hacker said when Travis got back to the table and filled them in. "I've run all the people you gave me. Braden Garrett's definitely a bad apple. He's got a wonderful string of arrests to his name, mostly for petty crimes, theft and making an unpleasant nuisance of himself. No proof he's the Shiny Man, though, but nothing that rules him out. Cleo has one citation for minor drugs, a couple of years ago, that she claimed were Braden's."

"Interesting," Jess said.

"Tracking down all of the major arrests Patricia's family members made is taking some time," Seth added, "but I'll get there. Harris Mitchell has a temper. He was charged with punching man in a bar when he was younger. Now he just makes a lot of complaints to the city's bylaw office that go nowhere and threatens a lot of lawsuits he doesn't file. Chief Peters has a couple of marks on his early career for sloppy police work, but nothing in well over a decade."

Travis's eyebrows rose. "You've been busy."

"It's what I do." Seth grinned. "I've also run both kindergarten teachers, the three preschool teachers and all four teacher's aids. All are clean and all are long-term Kilpatrick residents. Except our kindergarten teacher, Alvin Walker. The only crime he's committed is being way too whiny on social media about the fact that he couldn't afford the tuition to take this fancy master's degree program he was accepted into at Queen's University…

"Now, here's the cool thing." Seth held up his phone. A white map and a beige map shared the screen. A small red dot blinked on one map and a small blue dot blinked on the other.

"Willow and Dominic are wearing GPS-tracker anklets inside their socks and shoes," Seth continued. "Very discreet and pretty impossible to remove if you don't know how the fastening system works. It automatically sends me an alert if the child suffers any sudden jolt, like being grabbed or falling. And it means that there's no way either child is moving without my knowing exactly where they're going."

Seth took a deep breath and let it out theatrically.

"Finally," he said, "I've got Liam on standby, monitoring all the same things I am. He's also confirmed that he's now got a man undercover at the hospital with eyes on Patricia, and another undercover buddy nearby on call in case we need emergency backup."

Jess was thankful for Liam's help.

"Everything is as covered as it can be." Seth glanced at Travis. "Look, I know you hate leaving the kids anywhere. But as the guy who's guarding them, I can say with a hundred percent confidence that they're safer and better monitored here than they would be anywhere else in Kilpatrick."

"Thanks," Travis said.

Jess could practically see his heartstrings tearing.

She reached over and squeezed his fingers. "Hey," she said. "It's going to be okay. We'll be back before you know it."

"And nothing will make me happier than just sitting here and mucking about online until you return," Seth said. "Trust me. You have no idea how much I've missed just sitting in front of a screen."

They started for the front door but hadn't made it ten steps before the sound of a voice calling them made them stop and turn.

"Hey!" Alvin was striding toward them across the atrium. "I'm glad I caught you. Willow said somebody broke into the bookstore and threw all the books on the floor?"

Jess pressed his lips together as her mind spun through every conversation she'd had with the little girl or in front of her, praying that none of them had accidentally leaked anything important she could repeat.

"There was a break-in at the bookstore," Travis said. "Chief Peters is working on it."

"Have you talked to Cleo today?" Jess asked.

Alvin glanced at her, his eyes lingering on her face for a moment.

"I'm sorry, I saw you yesterday in all the chaos, and know who you are, but I don't think we've ever properly met." The teacher stretched out his hand for Jess's. She took it and they shook hands. "And no, I haven't talked to Cleo today. She sent me a few texts, but I haven't checked them yet because I was at work. We're not really..." He ran his hand through his hair. "I know people in this town think that Cleo and I are an item. But it's not serious. I went through a rough breakup recently, and I'm not really in a place right now where I'm ready to give my heart away until I'm sure it's right. Why? Is she okay?"

Jess could almost feel the air temperature drop as Travis took in a sharp breath. But all she said was, "I think you should call her." They turned to go. "It was nice to meet you."

"You, too," Alvin said. "Hope to see you at the school concert later. And if there's anything I can do to help out Patricia and the kids, let me know. Some of us were talking about having a community cleanup effort tomorrow, or maybe holding a big book sale at the store later this month and bringing the whole town together for a fund-raising flea market." Alvin half jogged, half ran back to the classroom.

Jess and Travis went to his truck, left the parking lot and started off on the road that led out of town. First the buildings and then the Welcome to Kilpatrick sign disappeared behind them.

"You've been quietly stewing to yourself for the past ten minutes," Jess said.

"I didn't think it was that long."

"It's been ever since Alvin talked to us," Jess said. "It's like you're judging him for not being a better whatever to Cleo, but at least he's not on his cell phone at work. I checked his wrist when he shook my hand and he doesn't have any bite marks. But, on the plus side, Seth has eyes on him, so if he suddenly decides to throw on a Shiny Man suit and run out to go do crimes, Seth will definitely notice."

"Funny," Travis said. "He has an alibi for Patricia's accident and the attack in my study. Not that there can't be more than one Shiny Man on the loose or a future copycat."

They passed a couple of mailboxes and then the last vestiges of town disappeared completely. Forest surrounded them. Towering trees and rocks lined the narrow rural highway.

"He was flirting with you," Travis added. "Even though he's got a thing going with Cleo and, as far as everyone in this town knows, you're my ex-fiancée."

"I'm your pretend ex-fiancée," Jess corrected, "and I don't get why you're so rattled by this."

"You never really noticed just how much guys flirted with you," Travis said. "Women usually don't."

Jess snorted. "You serious? Of course we notice! We just don't always like it and learn to tune it out, because most of the time it doesn't mean anything and a lot of the time it's insulting."

"Insulting?" Travis repeated. "How was it insulting to be constantly barraged by colleagues wanting to talk you out of whatever undercover case you were working on with me to go work with them?"

"Travis!" Her hands flew into the air and she was thankful he was the one driving. How could he be so obtuse? "You were always blunt with me, so I'm going to be really blunt with you.

"I'm a woman, in a male-dominated field, who's five foot two with naturally blond hair and blue eyes, who, because of my build and how much I exercise, am in relatively healthy shape. That means, to some guys, I fit into some idea of what they think of as 'cute' or 'pretty' or an accessory they can picture on their arm. None of that has anything to do with who I am as a person. It's insulting to me, to every woman who doesn't look like me, and to my badge."

Plus it had riled her up enough she'd been willing to go on probation over it. Travis eased the truck off the rural highway onto an even narrower road, with ragged edges. And she was thankful she hadn't tried to do the drive alone.

"But maybe you don't get it, because you were never like that," she added. "And I wasn't your type, so you didn't see me like that."

Now it was Travis's turn to snort.

"What do you mean, you weren't my type?" he asked. "What do you think my type is? You think I don't like strong, talented and intelligent women? Of course I found you attractive, very much so, but I also really respected you and didn't want to wreck our working relationship by putting you in an awkward position or coming across as a creep."

"Oh." She sat back against the seat, suddenly feeling the wind knocked from her. "Well, then, thank you for that."

He grinned. "No problem."

They hit a long, dirt and gravel road, wet with mud and dotted with puddles from rain that had fallen in the night. He eased up on the speed as a house appeared ahead, or rather, the remains of what had once been a house or even a converted barn.

She couldn't imagine what color the wood had been once, but now it was grayed from weather and disrepair. It's peaked, two-story roof caved in slightly on one side. Boards covered the broken windows. There wasn't another person or vehicle in sight.

"The Shiny Man's been getting his packages delivered here?" Jess asked.

"Apparently," Travis said. "If Seth is right."

"He almost always is."

He stopped the truck and they got out. Faint imprints of what had once been tire tracks streaked across the muddy ground. The long, wet grass that grew around the building was slightly flattened in a line leading to the front of the house.

"Either way, someone's been here recently," Jess added.

She made a quick call to Seth, checking that the kids were fine and confirming he had her and Travis's location on GPS, too, thanks to the trackers they had on their phones. Then she and Travis stood there for a long moment and stared at the house. The smell of impending rain filled the air. The farmhouse door hung ajar on broken hinges.

"So, we're going to go in there," Jess said.

"Apparently so." He glanced her way, and somehow, despite everything, she felt her chin rise and a determined grin cross her lips. There was something about having him there that always made her feel better, stronger, straightening her spine and filling her lungs with fresh air.

Travis reached into his pocket and pulled on a pair of gloves, waited until she put on hers, too, and then he reached across the gap between them and squeezed her hand. "I'm really glad you're here."

Yeah, so was she.

They approached the house slowly and cautiously. The damp wood of the front steps, sloped from decay, was soft underfoot.

Travis knocked twice on the door and it swung open to his touch. "Hello?"

There was no answer. They stepped into the gloom of what she guessed had once been a living room and the smell of damp wood and decay intensified. Thin, weak streams of light filtered in through the boarded-up windows.

Jess bent and brushed her hand across the floor.

"No dust," she noted. She stood. "Someone's been here."

But who and why?

They crossed the floor, moving deeper into the dark and empty room. Travis took a step forward and something clicked under his foot.

Sudden light flashed behind them, filling the empty room with blinding light.

Jess felt the air shift behind them and glanced back.

A shape clad in orange swung forward, flying at them seemingly from out of nowhere. She barely had a glimpse of a silver respirator mask and reflective jump-suit as the figure barreled into her, knocking her backward. She felt Travis catch her against his chest, his strong arms tightening around her.

Then Travis fell backward, taking Jess with him. They hit the floor and then fell through it, tumbling into darkness as a trap door opened up beneath them.

NINE

Darkness filled her eyes as they fell backward into cold, damp air. For a moment, Jess could feel Travis's arms around her. Then she fell from his grasp and there was nothing but the feeling of her body in free fall as the rectangular light of the trap door above them grew farther and farther away.

She heard the thud and grunt of Travis hitting the floor. Then a jarring jolt of pain shot through her as her own body hit the ground. She lay there for a moment, her winded lungs gasping. The faint sound of a rhythmic creak filtered down from above them as the silhouetted shape of a man moved back and forth in the light above them. The last glimmer of light disappeared in a crash as the trap door closed. There was nothing but pitch-black around her, the sound of her ragged breath escaping her lips and the smell of dirt filling her nostrils.

Help us, God! she prayed, battling the panic that threatened to overwhelm her. Her fingers brushed against first the phone in her pocket and then the weapon at her side. Were they alone? Was it safe to move? Would it be safe to yell? Then she heard Travis groan softly.

"Travis!" She gasped his name and rolled toward the sound.

"Jess," Travis's disembodied whisper echoed around her and filled her chest with hope.

"You okay?" she whispered back.

"Yeah." He groaned again. "Just sore all over. You?"

"Everything hurts, but I'm okay."

"Thank God," he said.

She felt her body bump against his. His warm breath brushed her face. Even in the darkness, she knew the scent of him anywhere, a mingling of pine deodorant, coffee and something else that was all him and felt like home. Her forehead bumped against his. "Do you think we're alone?"

He paused a long moment. "I think so, I can't hear anyone else or anything else really."

She closed her eyes and listened. Yeah, neither could she. But she'd still give it a moment before she raised her voice, switched on her phone's flashlight, or did anything other than lie there in pain, on the off chance somebody was listening or surveying them.

"Well, on the plus side," Travis said softly, "I can't think of anyone else I'd rather be trapped in a cellar with."

"You think it's a cellar?" she asked.

"Smells more musty than a basement, and I'm hoping calling it a dungeon would be oversell." His breath tickled her face. Travis's fingers looped through hers and they lay there a moment, side by side, waiting to catch their breaths.

"Trap door, huh?" Travis recovered first. "Haven't seen one of those since the raid on the tattoo parlor in Kingston."

"Yeah," she said, "but it's a whole lot different when you're staring at it from the other side."

"Have I told you how amazing it's been to have someone around who knows about that side of my life?" he asked. "As much as I've loved my life in Kilpatrick, parts of it have been incredibly lonely. Now, if we've gone this long with no one barging in or attacking us, I'm going to risk moving." She felt him pull away from her in the darkness.

"Good news is, it seems safe to sit up," he said. There was another shuffling noise. "And stand," he added.

She felt his hand reach for hers again. She took it and let him help pull her to her feet.

"Now," Travis said, "let's hope at least one of our phones survived the fall."

Agreed. As she was pulling her phone from her pocket, she saw a light flicker to her right. She looked over. Travis's face glanced back at her, illuminated in the pale glow of his cell phone screen.

"More good news, we've got light," he said.

"Is there more bad news?" she asked.

"Yup, no phone signal."

She turned her phone on and found it was the same on both counts.

Travis waved his phone's flashlight around the room, if they could call it that. It was barely ten feet wide and roughly square. The walls were made of old, red brick that was faded and chipped in the corners. The ground was packed dark earth. The ceiling above was low, barely inches above Travis's head, which was surprising and far lower than she'd have expected considering how far the fall had seemed.

"I'm guessing this is a subbasement," she said.

One with no exits, no windows and no doors, besides the narrow chute they'd fallen through.

She steeled a breath and kept looking. "So, we're agreed that this was a trap, right?" Jess asked.

"Afraid so," Travis said.

She closed her eyes and tried to remember what she'd seen.

"I didn't even see where he came from," she said eventually, opening her eyes. "Did you?"

"No."

Fear pounded in her chest as they searched the exit-less room. What was this criminal's plan? To kill them? To leave them there and let them starve? But she knew, even as she thought the questions, that she didn't need to speak them. Travis would be thinking them, too, chasing question after question down even worse rabbit holes than she could imagine, until one of them finally spoke the words they both needed to hear.

"It doesn't matter what he wants with us," Jess said. "All that matters is getting out alive."

"I was just thinking that," Travis said.

"So, what's the plan?" she asked.

"Well, presumably this room was originally built with some kind of entrance and exit before the trap door was installed," he said, "and I don't know about you, but I don't want to try climbing up that chute."

Not even if there hadn't been a closed trap door and the potential of whoever trapped them waiting at the top. "Me neither."

"Didn't think so," he said, turning toward the walls. "I'm going to figure out where there might have been an exit. Can you hold both phones for maximum light?"

"Absolutely."

She took his phone and held one in each hand, then stood back and watched as he methodically searched the walls, feeling the bricks, pulling at them, and tapping the walls with his knuckles, until finally he found a patch that seemed newer than the rest. Then he pulled his knife from his pocket, slid it between the bricks and started prying. And so began the very long and tedious job of slowly digging their way out of captivity.

Travis and Jess went back and forth, between one prying the bricks out inch by inch, while the other held the light, eventually cutting down to just one phone and switching each one off in turn to preserve the battery life.

In an odd way, it was like a physical representation of the work they'd done back at their desks, side by side, in near silence, taking down criminals. They'd spent hours and hours each day, for days, weeks and even months, combing over evidence, websites, phone records, photographs and videos, slowly compiling the data needed to track criminals and bring them to justice. Like prying bricks free from the cement holding them together to form a wall, it was painstaking and exhausting work.

"I'm sorry I didn't realize how bad a toll the job used to take on you," Jess said. "Now that I'm reminded of it, I remember how irritable, overtired and jumpy you used to be. Guess I'd forgotten all that."

"Guess there's nothing wrong with remembering the best side of someone," Travis said. The tip of his knife moved slowly around the edge of the next brick.

"It's just…if I'd known, maybe I could've done something to help," Jess said.

Travis paused and looked at her over his shoulder.

"Don't worry, Jess," he said. "There isn't a doubt in my mind that you would've been the first person in my corner helping me." He turned back. "You'd have tried to do everything the Tatlow family did for me and more. But how were you supposed to help me with something when I didn't even realize there was a problem? You can't be expected to help save someone who doesn't even know he needs saving."

Travis's knife scraped over the cement with an eerie, high-pitched sound that seemed to echo through the prison they were trapped in. How long would the Shiny Man leave them there? What would they face when they escaped?

"The kids are okay," she said after a long moment. "I'm sure of it. Seth has eyes on them in person, Liam is monitoring them remotely, and they're in an environment where they're surrounded by people in the community who know them. If anyone so much as slams a door too loudly or knocks over a stack of books near those kids, my team will spring into action."

"I know," Travis said. There was a weariness to his

voice tinged with worry. And she suspected he'd been praying for Willow and Dominic just as much and as relentlessly as she had been.

"I read through your entire case file on the Chimera last night," he added, "and the details of your upcoming undercover operation."

"And?" she asked.

He paused longer than she would've liked and then, when he started talking again, he did so without meeting her eyes.

"It's solid," Travis said. "Really solid. Not that I'm surprised. You've always been an incredible cop. I can't think of a single thing you could improve on it. I just wish you wouldn't do it."

"Because you think it's too risky," Jess pressed.

"Because I don't want to lose you again." Travis's voice rose, only slightly, but enough that the sound seemed to echo around her. "The only way the Chimera is going to let you get close enough to see his face is if he thinks he can hurt you and use you. And once you get inside his web, it won't be easy to escape. Losing you the first time hurt too much and while I get that this is your job and you're really good at it, I don't want to lose you again. Especially like this."

There was a clink as another piece of brick broke off in front of him. Travis tossed it aside and then slid his hand through the hole. The wall was at least three bricks thick, but it seemed like they'd finally broken through. Jess felt a breath of relief leave her lungs. But an odd tightness still filled her chest that had nothing to do with the subbasement they were trapped in.

Travis reached for the cell phone. She handed it to him and he shone the light through the opening.

"Okay, we've got an empty room, with a window." He let out a sigh that matched hers. "We're going to get out."

He handed back the phone and started working on making the hole bigger.

"I really wish I had a better option for taking down the Chimera," Travis said. "I've been racking my brain trying to find one and I have to admit I think your approach is smart. If not you, then we'd have to find somebody else to go in undercover, and there's no time to get someone up to speed on all the Chimera's operations. The only other person who could do it would be me, and my cover's already blown. It would make more sense to leak my location and wait for his henchmen to come find me."

He ran his hand over the back of his head, spreading even more dirt through his dusty hair. "You know I'd do it. I'd put my life on the line to stop the Chimera and save you."

"But Willow and Dominic need you," Jess said. "Patricia will need you, too, when she wakes up. You have a life and a family here." And she had no one depending on her.

Travis nodded and went back to chipping away at the wall.

She could hear thunder faintly rumbling in the distance now, mingling with the sound of water trickling. More rain was coming.

"Even if it wasn't for the kids," Travis continued, "it would still be wrong for me to be your handler."

"Because of your history with the Chimera?" she asked.

"No, because I'd be emotionally compromised." Travis turned around and looked at her full-on in the eyes. "I have feelings for you, Jess. Real, strong, deep feelings. I have for a really long time, longer than I can remember."

She felt her lips part. But his hands raised palms-up before she could speak.

"And no," he added, "I'm not about to stand around here in some creepy criminal's dungeon trying to analyze what kinds of feelings they are and what that could mean for us. So, please don't ask me that. Because it won't matter to what happens next. The courses of our lives are set. And we've got more important things to worry about than what kinds of emotions two people, who once worked together, once felt. Just know that they were real and they never went away, no matter how much time we've spent apart."

He took a step back and her phone light illuminated the hole. It was now three feet wide.

"Now, do you want to go first or second?" he asked.

She swallowed hard, feeling all the words he'd just spoken pile up unacknowledged around them like the cast-off pieces of brick surrounding them on the floor.

"You go first," she said, finally. "I'm the one with a gun."

"My thoughts, too," Travis said. "See you on the other side."

An uncertain smile crossed his lips, which she suspected had far more to do with what he'd just admitted than whatever lay on the other side. He turned and crawled through.

Jess waited and prayed, watching his torso then his legs and finally his boots disappear through the hole. There was silence for a breath. Then Travis's face appeared in the opening.

"Okay," he said. "We're good."

She passed him the phones and edged her way into the small, square room. There was a metal door without a doorknob on their side. The walls were made of concrete and there was a window set high above in one of them. She could hear the heavy rain beating against the pane.

"I'll hoist you up," Travis said, his hands brushing her forearms. Then she felt him push the keys to his truck into her hand. "You can climb up onto my shoulders. Hopefully you'll be able to get the window open, but if not, there are plenty of broken bricks lying around. Get out, call Seth, and get help. Get to the kids and make sure they're okay, and then come back for me."

"No." Her head shook. "Don't be ridiculous. I'm not leaving without you. You can pile up bricks to make a stool. I'll find some big rocks and toss them down to you. I'll search the vehicle for rope or something. I'm not leaving you here and I'm not going anywhere without you."

"Jess," Travis pointed out, "there's a criminal on the loose, who kidnapped us and threw us in a cellar."

"Yeah, I know." She tossed her hair around her shoulders. "And again, I'm not about to leave you down here, in a hole, to face him alone. I'm…"

She swallowed hard, feeling a dozen words she'd never dreamed admitting to herself, let alone blurting out to him, cross her heart and mind.

"I'm emotionally compromised, too, Travis," she said. "I have been for a lot longer than I'd like to admit. So I'm not about to just take off and leave you. We do this together and we don't split up. Got it?"

For a long moment they just stood there, face-to-face, not saying anything. She could hear their breaths echoing around them in the gloom, the rain beating down on the window above them and thunder rumbling in the distance.

Then Travis's hands reached up and brushed the sides of Jess's face.

"I was never good enough for you," he said. His voice grew husky in his throat. "And even if I'm a better man now, it's too late for us with whatever it is we think we're feeling."

"I know." Jess nodded. "But I'm still not about to save myself and leave here without you."

"I get that." Travis lowered his face to hers, she raised hers to his and their lips met. They kissed, sliding their arms around each other and hugging for one long moment like they never wanted to let go. Then, without a word, Travis swept her up into his arms and lifted her high above his head. Her heart pounded in her chest. Her toes brushed against his shoulders. His hands steadied her legs.

She reached for the window, pulled the latch back so hard it snapped off in her hands. Using it like a lever, she forced the window open. Rain lashed against her face.

Wind howled in toward her. Then she felt Travis grab her feet and raise her high above his head. She slithered through the window and crawled out onto the grass.

"Hang on," she called down. "I'll get you out of there."

A twig cracked to her right. She scrambled to her knees. A man in a red plaid shirt and jeans stood over her. There was a rifle in his hand. The flashlight in the other shone in her eyes.

"Travis!" she shouted, reaching for her weapon as she rose. "Stay down!"

"Jessica?" The voice was male, strong and young. "Don't shoot! I'm... I'm Nick Henry. Liam sent me!"

The pool of light dropped to the ground by her side. The young man was in his early to mid twenties, she guessed, with earnest eyes and trim blond hair.

Her grasp tightened on her weapon. "Show me your badge!" she demanded.

"No badge, ma'am," Nick said. "I'm not law enforcement. I'm just a random guy who got a call from an old buddy I owed a favor to, asking me to drop by a property and make sure everyone was safe."

Right. And she was the Queen of England. Whoever Nick Henry was, he was someone she'd never heard Liam mention before but apparently felt confident calling in an emergency.

"Liam told me to tell you that the children and Seth are safe," Nick added, rain pouring down his face. "That there's no change in Patricia's condition or any sign of trouble at the hospital. Also, Liam's sorry he forgot to water your plants on the office windowsill."

Yeah, that sounded like Liam.

"If you know Liam, what's the name of his cat?" she asked.

"That's a trick question," Nick said. "Liam's convinced all cats have something against him. He also told me that he and Seth made the call to let Willow perform in the school concert, figuring it was safer and less suspicious than trying to take the kids anywhere. But it starts in forty-five minutes and if you and Travis don't make it in time, you'll be in major trouble."

Yeah, that sounded about right, too. She dropped the weapon and stretched out her hand. "Nice to meet you," she said.

"Likewise." He shook it.

Was he a cop? A detective? His bearing definitely exuded authority and responsibility.

"I hope that popping by to help us out didn't cause too big a problem in whatever else you've got going on," Jess said.

"No problem," Nick told her. "I'd do anything for Liam. He saved my life once."

Yeah, a lot of people felt that way about him.

"You got rope?" she asked. "We've got to get Travis out of the basement, and since the window seems safe and the house seemed booby-trapped, it's the safest way to do it."

He nodded. "In my truck."

"Good," she said then asked, "I take it there are no hostiles on the property?"

Nick shook his head. "No, ma'am," he said. "But we've got what looks like a dead body."

* * *

Eight minutes later, Travis stood beside Jess and Nick in the doorway of the dilapidated house and watched as an orange-clad figure in a silver respirator mask swung back and forth, suspended by a rope from the ceiling.

He glanced at the young man Liam had sent to find them when they'd gone dark, who'd helped haul him out of the basement window.

"You tried to identify the body?" Travis asked.

"No, sir." Nick shook his head. "I'd been here less than five minutes before I found you both. I found the door open, called Liam, did a perimeter search and found Jess almost immediately. I could tell by the angle of the man's neck that if he had been alive, he was now dead, and from his build that he wasn't either of the people I'd been sent here to find. I imagine you'd like to be gone by the time police get here?"

"Yes, thank you," Travis said. "It will all depend on whether we're dealing with a suicide or a murder."

Sometimes it felt like he was holding on to his secret identity by a thread. But with God's help, Travis was going to cling to it as long as he could. As for Nick, was he RCMP? Ontario Provincial Police?

No, that didn't quite seem to fit.

Travis crossed his arms. "You're military, aren't you?" Travis asked.

Nick nodded. "Yup, but I grew up with two older brothers who do what you do for a living, so I'm very used to the drill."

A military man who'd grown up with undercover detectives? Interesting. He'd come across a couple of incredible "Detective Henrys" before and wondered if this young man was related to them. Although, if he was, he'd probably know his brothers' work well enough to deny it.

"And what exactly is it that you think I do?" Travis knew he shouldn't pry but couldn't help himself.

"I have no idea," Nick said cheerfully.

Sounded about right. Despite the seriousness of the situation, Travis was suddenly and unexpectedly reminded of one of the things he had enjoyed, very much, about being a cop that he'd forgotten. He missed the camaraderie, especially in undercover work, among strangers who came together to have each other's backs and save lives. He'd been so hard on Jess's team and now he shuddered to think where he would've been without them.

"Looks like the place is booby-trapped," Travis said. He glanced over to Jess, who was now standing on the only dry patch of the porch, on a group video chat with Seth and Liam. "I'm going to check the body."

Jess nodded. "Stay safe."

Travis took the high-powered flashlight that Nick offered him and started slowly across the floor, sweeping light over every corner as he went. Now that he knew what he was looking for, it was all so simple to see. There was a trip wire, a pulley system, the trap door, plus a few other suspiciously uneven floor tiles or loose wires that he was careful to avoid. Whoever had been using this abandoned house to collect Shiny Man packages had certainly made sure it was rigged to trap or kill anyone poking around inside it.

He crossed the floor gingerly, reached the body and pulled the mask back. Sadness swelled deep inside his heart.

It was Braden Garrett.

Their prime suspect. Cleo's ex-boyfriend—whom she'd said had been harassing her and whom the chief of police was going to help her file a protective order against—was now dead.

He peeled back the corner of the man's right glove. Sure enough, he could see Jess's self-defense bite marks from the night before on his wrist.

So, the Shiny Man who'd ambushed Patricia, attacked him in his apartment and tried to drug and kidnap Jess in the woods was dead.

By what looked like suicide.

His detective's gaze swept over the man's features and then he leaned in and sniffed the sickly sweet scent that was faint but unmistakable.

No, Travis didn't believe Braden had taken his own life for an instant.

He glanced back, Jess's eyes met his and, even without him saying a word, her eyes widened and her fingers rose to her lips.

"Victim is Braden Garrett," he said. His head shook slowly as he walked back across the floor toward her. "My guess, based on a preliminary glance of skin color and bruising pattern, is that he was sedated, most likely with chloroform judging by the smell, and then had his neck broken. Didn't suffer, had absolutely no idea what was happening to him, and died in his sleep."

And despite his criminal record and being an all-around

not great guy, who clearly scared his ex-girlfriend, he was still a human being whose life someone had taken from him. Anger crashed over Travis, engulfing the sorrow.

"Call Liam and tell him to get someone we trust on this," he said to Nick. "Make sure whoever he calls knows that a former RCMP detective has suspicions it's a homicide disguised to look like a suicide and to take a close look at the evidence. Local police will definitely need to be looped in on this, too. District Police Chief Peters of Kilpatrick was already in the process of helping the dead man's former girlfriend obtain a protective order. I don't trust Peters as far as I can chuck him, but he needs to know."

Travis stepped out onto the porch and walked over to Jess and Nick.

"Wrist injury indicates he's probably the man who attacked Jess outside the farmhouse last night," Travis added "I don't know who killed him, or why, but I don't believe this is over. I just… My gut tells me this isn't over."

"Understood," Nick said. He took out his phone, dialed and was talking to someone almost instantly.

Travis leaned toward Jess. "Do you think we can trust him to secure the crime scene?"

"I think the fact Liam trusted him enough to call him is good enough for me," Jess said. She glanced at her phone. "Liam already has a team of people on the way to secure the scene now, and we have half an hour to get to Willow's concert performance. Seth says he'll pick Dominic up from the nursery and save us seats."

Travis's head spun. His brain had whiplash from trying to be too many people at once. They might've just survived a trap, dug their way out of a dungeon and uncovered a body, but Willow would never forgive him if he missed her playing the triangle.

"Yeah, we got to go," Travis said. He turned to Nick, who was now on a video call with Liam. "Thank you for your help. Both of you." He nodded to Liam on the screen, who nodded back. "Thank you for coming to our rescue."

"I'm just a soldier who got lost, happened upon a body and called the cops to handle it," Nick said with a smile as he stepped forward, keeping his phone screen tilted so Liam could stay in the conversation.

Travis shook Nick's hand, hoping he'd meet the man again one day in the future.

"I'll take care of it," Liam said. "We've already got people en route. It's all good."

"Thank you," Travis said again. "I owe you one." Probably several more than one.

Liam nodded.

Travis jogged to his truck, Jess one step beside him.

"How long have we got?" he asked.

"Twenty-eight minutes," she said. "Fortunately, Seth says he told Alvin that we were running a bit late and he agreed to try to push it. Not that Alvin is running the show, but he can always make the kids walk slow."

Travis was thankful for that. He opened his door and climbed inside.

"Any idea what cover story Seth gave Alvin?" Travis asked.

Jess climbed in on the passenger's side and did up her seat belt.

"Seth told Alvin that you and I went for a long romantic hike to see about rekindling our romantic relationship, got caught in the rain and had to take shelter somewhere with no cell phone reception service."

Travis chuckled and made a mental note to thank Seth for that.

Jess pulled her sun visor down and looked at herself in the mirror. She frowned.

"Well, at least that will make it easier to explain why we showed up at the school concert looking like I was just dredged from a pond," she quipped.

Travis reached across the center console and grabbed her hand.

"You're beautiful," he said. "You were always beautiful, back in the day, but now you're more gorgeous than ever."

"You've seen me in party dresses and ball gowns," she said. "For our undercover sting at the ambassador's gala in Ottawa, I had a hairdresser, makeup artist and fashion designer. And you wait to tell me I'm pretty until I'm soaked?"

"I waited until after we'd both blurted out something about feelings," he said.

And with the reminder of how short life was, he was going to grasp every moment he could.

Jess didn't answer. She just looped her fingers through his and held his hand tightly. And despite everything that was happening, there was an odd lightness in his chest, like he'd been carrying an invisible weight and had somehow, finally, been able to let it go. His heart was still so heavy. There'd been no improvement with Patricia's condition and right now police investigators would be going over the scene of the abandoned house, alerting Braden Garrett's family of his death and investigating his murder.

In less than twenty-four hours, Jess would be leaving his life to go undercover to face a ruthless criminal and he had no idea if he'd ever see her again. And yet, somehow, the fact that he'd admitted having feelings for her and was now holding her hand, made the incredible heaviness surrounding him a little bit easier to take.

After a while, Jess pulled her hand from his and busied herself with checking in with Liam and Seth. Seemed the RCMP team had arrived at the crime scene. A car with a broken headlight that had been registered to Braden Garrett had been found hidden in the woods not far from the house. It matched the description of the one that had followed them the night before.

The sign for Kilpatrick loomed ahead. He steered toward the civic center and prayed for the investigation into Braden's death. He begged God to heal Patricia and to find a way to keep Willow and Dominic in his life. Then Travis glanced sideways at the beautiful, strong and incredible woman now sitting beside him.

And, Lord, please be with Jess. Keep her safe, successful and happy. Help her take down the Chimera and countless more criminals. Fill her life with joy, happiness and love.

Even if he couldn't be the man who was standing there beside her doing so.

The civic center's parking lot was full and he didn't much feel like parking his truck somewhere he was likely to be caught in a traffic jam trying to get out. So instead he parked on a nearby side street. He and Jess

cleaned themselves up the best they could with the tow-
els, hand wipes and bottled water he had in his truck.

His hand linked with Jess's as they dashed for the
civic center and he wasn't even sure if he'd grabbed her
hand first or if she'd been the first one to reach for him.
All he knew was they were running, hand in hand, as
they mounted the steps and then waited for a moment
to be buzzed in by a security guard.

They reached the auditorium just as final strains
of the grade six band's rendition of the national an-
them were playing. Travis scanned the room. He didn't
see Chief Peters, Harris or Cleo anywhere. Surely,
Liam would make sure someone informed the chief of
Braden's death. Had he been called to the crime scene?

Seth was sitting in the back row, Dominic in his
arms, and empty seats he was zealously guarding on
both sides. Jess squeezed Travis's hand once and let go.
Then they crossed the floor toward Seth, saying a quiet
hello to Travis's friends and neighbors as they went.

"Hey," Travis said softly, tapping Seth on the shoulder. "Thanks for…everything."

"No problem," Seth whispered. He glanced from Travis to Jess as they and the audience took their seats. "I'm
just glad you made it back alive in one piece. Even if
you do look like you just got tossed off the ark."

Travis opened his arms for Dominic to wriggle happily into them. He hugged the baby boy to his chest and
took a deep breath, breathing him in. Then the stage
lights came on and he watched as the kindergarten class
shuffled onto the stage.

Willow's huge eyes scanned the crowd. Her lip quivered as she took her place at the end of the wooden risers and Travis knew she hadn't seen them.

Suddenly, Jess leaped to her feet, quickly and impulsively waving both of her hands above her head. Willow saw her and a huge smile crossed her face. Jess sat back down as Willow's eyes flitted to Travis, Dominic and Seth. He watched as she gave them a little wave. Then Willow took a deep breath and her class started singing.

There were over two dozen children up on stage— singing loudly and enthusiastically shaking, banging, waving or pounding various percussion instruments— and what felt like half the town crowded into the auditorium. But he only had eyes for Willow and she only had eyes for them.

Confidence filled Willow's face. Joy shone in her eyes as she smacked the little triangle confidently and firmly when it was her turn, in time to the music.

He glanced from Willow up on stage to Dominic and then to Jess, and suddenly, in a flash, Travis saw the perfect life he'd always longed for but had never even let himself dream he could have. He saw himself as the father to a bold, inquisitive, smart daughter like Willow and a happy, playful son like Dominic. He saw himself as a member of a vibrant, small-town community, where everybody knew him and they cared for his family and he cared for theirs. He saw himself with the only woman he'd ever loved by his side as his partner and his wife.

The song ended, people started clapping and Travis leaped to his feet, trying to cradle Dominic with one hand and clap awkwardly by slapping his free hand on his own elbow. And he knew, with absolute certainty, this was what he wanted the rest of his life to be, even if he had no hope of ever getting there.

In the past twenty-four hours, nothing and everything had changed. Patricia had asked him to become the children's legal guardian, but he couldn't while living under a fake identity. He'd confessed he had feelings for Jess, held her in his arms and kissed her lips, but she was still leaving his life tomorrow. Even if he had the courage to tell her how he felt, how could he ever ask her to give up her entire life to live under a secret identity with him?

It was impossible. And yet, as he stood there in the auditorium and watched as Willow and the kids disappeared backstage with her class, he knew, for the first time in his life, where he belonged and what he wanted his future to be.

He turned to Seth. "I should have recorded that for Patricia."

"Don't worry." Seth chuckled. "I did."

The lights went out with the crack of dozens of fluorescent lights switching off at once. Voices shouted. Chairs tumbled over as people jumped to their feet. But above it all, Travis could somehow hear the one little voice he'd know anywhere.

Willow was screaming.

Seth grabbed his arm and pushed his cell phone before his eyes. He looked down at a small, blinking red light in a sea of lines and boxes, and it took Travis a moment to realize what he was looking at.

"Willow's alarm alert has been activated and her GPS is moving!" Seth said. "Someone's abducted her!"

TEN

Jess watched as Travis's terrified face went ashen in the dim light of the cell phone. She sprang to her feet and snatched the phone tracker from Seth's hand.

"I'm going after her!" Jess shouted.

"No! I am—" Travis started to argue, but she cut him off.

"You need to protect Dominic!" she said. "I'm armed. Stay with Seth. Alert the team. Keep Dominic safe! I'll go after Willow!"

"Take this!" Seth shoved an earpiece into her hand and she didn't have time to wonder where he'd pulled one from so quickly.

"You got another way to track her?" she asked. "Like a backup phone?"

"Of course!" Seth said. "I'll be watching you both."

She turned to go when she felt Travis's lips brush the top of her head.

"Stay safe," he said.

"You, too," she replied. "I'll bring her back safe, I promise."

Jess turned and ran for the side door of the auditorium, making her way through the crowd in the darkness as it surged around her. It was pandemonium. Children were crying, parents were trying to quiet them and staff was yelling for everyone to stay calm and in their seats, that the power would be back on soon.

In the meantime, she was certain, that whoever had cut the power had one target and one target only. And Jess was going to find and rescue her.

She burst through the door and ended up in an empty foyer. Dark hallway spread in both directions. She paused for a second and prayed, waiting for the small map on Seth's phone to center itself and tell her which way to go. Then the lines stopped spinning and she realized what she was looking at. It was an overlay of a blueprint of the building with a blinking dot showing where Willow was.

Jess turned and ran down the hallway, hit another junction, paused to check the screen, then turned right and kept running. The sound of the auditorium faded behind her. The hallway grew darker ahead. The sound of her own pounding feet and racing heart filled her ears.

Then she heard it. Willow was screaming from somewhere up ahead.

Hold on, Willow! I'm coming!

She pressed on, feeling the sound of Willow's voice filling her with fresh determination, strength and drive. She rounded another corner.

"Jess!" Willow shouted.

Jess barely had time to dart her gaze to the floor to

shield her eyes as a sudden light flashed and bounced off the glass windows of the classroom around her. Then it stopped and Jess looked up through the haze of light and darkness, forcing her painful, watering eyes to focus on the shapes ahead of her.

The Shiny Man stood before her, clad in his orange reflective jumpsuit and eerie buglike silver respirator mask. He had one arm around Willow, lifting her up off the ground as he dragged her backward.

"Jess!" Willow screamed. "Help me!"

Help me, Lord! I can't see!

The Shiny Man was getting away.

"No! Stop! Put me down!" Willow's desperate cries seemed to echo around her.

"Jess!" Seth's voice was in her ear. "There's a door behind him! He's about to leave the building!"

She had to stop him. No matter what it took and no matter what sacrifice she had to make. He was not going to take that little girl.

She yanked her weapon from her holster. "Stop! Police!"

Through light and shadows, she saw Shiny Man pause, falter in his steps.

"I'm not playing! Let her go!" Jess's voice rose, filling the space around them with a strength as it rose to crescendo. "Right now! Or I'll shoot!"

Already her vision was recovering. Blobs and blurs of light and darkness were sharpening before her eyes. She steadied her weapon with both hands, praying for an opportunity to take the shot. If he turned to run, she'd shoot his leg. If he shifted Willow to the side, she'd take out his opposite shoulder. Whatever it took to keep him from taking Willow.

The little girl's cries had dropped to whimpers.

Jess gritted her teeth and prayed she wouldn't have to shoot for Willow's sake.

"Jess!" Seth's voice crackled in her ear again. "There's a van with its motor running just outside the door."

Shiny Man took another step backward.

"I'm Detective Jessica Eddington of the Royal Canadian Mounted Police!" she shouted, feeling her voice rise to its full strength and power until it filled the hallway. "You're not going to get a warning shot. You hurt one hair on that girl's head and you will not make it out of here alive. Now, let Willow go!"

The Shiny Man hesitated a second. Then, as she watched, Willow fell from his grasp and he turned and ran.

Jess scrambled forward, holstering her weapon just as Willow launched herself into Jess's arms. She caught the little girl to her chest and cradled her tightly. The emergency door slammed shut ahead of her. Shiny Man was gone. But for now, all that mattered was that Willow was safe.

"I've got her," Jess told Seth. "He got away but I've got Willow."

"Thank You, God!" Travis's voice filled her ear and she wondered if Seth had another earpiece or if they were somehow sharing one. "Stay there! We're coming to you."

"Understood," she said.

She sank to the ground, her legs suddenly feeling weak as all the adrenaline that had propelled her forward now seemed to crash down on her.

Then she felt Willow's tear-stained cheek press against hers. Her voice came out staccato through sobs. "You…saved…me…from…the…Shiny Man."

"I did," Jess said. She held her close. "And I'm so glad you're safe. Your baby brother's with Travis and Seth, and they're coming to find us. Everything's going to be okay."

Willow's face filled hers, her eyes wide. "Jess," she said, "you're a police woman?"

The lights flickered on. The power was back. Jess looked up as Travis and Seth, now holding Dominic, pelted around the corner toward them.

Prayers of thanksgiving poured from Travis's lips as he dropped to the ground and wrapped his arms around Willow, scooping her up and holding her tightly. Then Travis looked at Jess over the top of Willow's head, tears glistening in the corners of his eyes.

"Thank you." Emotion choked his voice in his throat until it was barely more than a whisper. "Thank you for saving her!"

"You're welcome," Jess said, slowly, taking Seth's hand as he helped her up. She glanced from Seth to Travis, her heart pounding in her chest as the full weight of what had just happened hit her. "But I just blew my cover."

"Look, I'm sorry, Jess, but you and Seth have to leave as soon as possible," Liam said, his face was grim on

Seth's laptop video screen. "You don't need me to tell you this, but with your cover blown, there's no choice."

Travis looked down at the wood grain of Patricia's table. Night had fallen, the children were in bed and Jess was seated beside him, but he didn't look at her face. He didn't know how to. His heart was so heavy, he could barely breathe.

The mood had been somber as they'd returned to the house. Dinner had been take-out pizza, and Jess had gotten changed while Travis had done the bedtime routine alone. Seth's duplicate box of Shiny Man's order had arrived and was now spread out over the table. All night, the fact that Jess had blown her cover had been buzzing around in the back of his mind like an insect he didn't want to swat at in case it stung him.

Instead he'd focused on how incredibly thankful he was that Willow was back safe and unharmed. But now, with the children asleep in the room above, and sitting around the table talking to the team, the full weight of what had happened and what it meant had finally hit him like a heavy stone landing in his gut.

"I'm sorry," Jess said. Her eyes flitted from Liam's face on the screen to Travis's and back again. "My vision was compromised. He was holding a minor child. It was the only way—"

"Nobody is blaming you," Liam cut in, his voice firm. "You made a call in a high-pressure situation in order to protect a minor child. It was unfortunate, but necessary."

Was it, though? Travis thought. He definitely wouldn't have ever doubted her before. She was way too good a cop for anything other than the benefit of the doubt. But believing in his heart that she'd made the right call somehow didn't make it any easier to look her in the eye and know what she'd cost them. Or maybe it was just knowing that his dreams were going up in smoke.

"I'm going to recap," Liam said. "I think as a team it would be helpful to take a look at the whole unvarnished situation, besides outside of what all of us might want, hope or wish it to be.

"We have one victim of a suspected homicide, Braden Garret. He was found dressed as the so-called Shiny Man and, we have every reason to believe, has been posing as the Shiny Man for several attacks, including on a current and former undercover detective. We have a second Shiny Man who attempted to abduct Willow today. We also have two minor children who've been living in close proximity to someone in witness protection and are now in his care, after their only living relative was attacked by Braden, while he was posing as the Shiny Man. Their primary caregiver and only living relative is now in a coma."

With no signs of improvement, no matter how many times Travis called the hospital to check, or how many prayers he and others in the community prayed.

"One of the minor children just survived an abduction attempt," Liam continued. "Although a police report has been filed and the child is now safe, we also have doubts about whether the local district police chief can be trusted and therefore he has not been fully briefed on the situation. All correct so far?"

"Yes," Travis said. "Correct."

Travis wasn't sure if hearing what was happening to his life laid bare in a police briefing helped or hurt. But at least Liam was getting the facts right.

"An undercover detective chose to blow her cover to save a minor child from abduction by this secondary Shiny Man," Liam added. "We still have no idea who this individual is, who murdered the other Shiny Man, if the two Shiny Men were working together or what possible motive there is for any of these attacks." He sighed. "Anything I'm missing?"

"The bookstore was ransacked," Jess said. "There's talk of a community effort to restore it, but still it feels like maybe the property was a target. Willow seems convinced that the Shiny Man is after her books."

"Because Willow loves her books," Travis said quickly. "They're her favorite things. That and her brother."

And her community, and her class, and her family. All of which he was now afraid she and her baby brother were all going to lose.

"It's still a potential data point," Jess said.

"It's not a data point," Travis said. "It's a little girl's life."

He immediately felt bad for being sharp. But at the same time, this was what he hated about the job and this is what had killed him about it—looking at real people's lives and treating them like statistics. Even though he knew there was good reason why detectives like him were trained to keep their emotional distance from the people whose lives they were trying to save. But Willow wasn't a case. She and her brother were family.

"I think I've figured out how the Shiny Man was able to be inside the civic center without setting off the metal detectors," Seth said after a long pause, the kind of hesitation in his voice that implied he was scanning the ground for eggshells.

"I've gone through everything he's ordered and done my best to recreate his getup," Seth continued. "Looks like he took the guts of a tactical light and implanted them in a standard mini plastic flashlight, which got him past security. He also wore special contact lenses that reduced the light's glare. They're not a perfect fix, so I'm guessing he also closed his eyes at strategic moments when he set off the light to give him an advantage. Nothing all that special, honestly. He was just really smart in how he used it."

Which got them where, exactly? Nowhere they hadn't been twenty-four hours ago.

"Jess and Seth," Liam said, "do what you can to help gather evidence and set up any additional security features you're working on, and then head back to rendezvous with the team in Ottawa. I know you hate to cut and run without catching this guy. Trust me, I do, too. But with Jess's cover blown, it's the safest option.

"As for Travis and the kids, we're going to get an extraction team to pick you guys up and take you to a safe house in Sudbury to be near Patricia in the hospital. My first choice will be to send a helicopter, but we might need to send a van depending who's available.

We'll loop social services in to meet you at the hospital. Give me an hour."

Travis's head shot up. "You're going to extract the children from their home in the middle of the night?"

"Do you have a better option?" Liam asked. "I can push it to just before dawn so that they get some sleep but leave under cover of darkness. The most important thing we can do right now is to make sure the children are taken care of."

"I will find a better option," Travis said. "I'll take care of them."

"With all due respect, you don't exist!" Liam said, and for the first time since Travis had met the steady and solid man on video screen, the detective's voice rose. "You're an imaginary person whose identity was created by a very dedicated team of Witness Protection agents—including myself. And I get it." Liam let out a long breath and his voice dropped just as suddenly as it had risen. "Trust me, I'm not unsympathetic. In fact, as someone who has been undercover many, many times, I know what it's like to lose yourself inside another identity and begin to think that's who you are."

Unexpected pain flashed in Liam's eyes, like something long deeply hidden had floated to the surface.

"But you have to remember that isn't really you," Liam continued. "And, again, as much as I hate to say this, you weren't supposed to get as close to that family as you did. These people you care about don't know who you really are."

Okay, but maybe Travis had no idea who he was anymore, either. He wasn't the man he'd been when he'd first entered Witness Protection. He wasn't the man who'd driven himself to exhaustion, living on caffeine with no real relationships and no peace in his heart. And while Travis Stone of Kilpatrick, Ontario, with friends, community and an unexpected family, wasn't him, either, it was the happiest and closest to being real he'd ever been.

And with him gone, and all that gone, who was he now?

ELEVEN

Jess wasn't surprised when Travis slipped away upstairs as they wrapped up the conversation. She could hardly blame him for wanting to spend as much time as he could with the children. Seth ended the video call and went back to whatever he was searching for on his computer. She stretched out on the pullout couch in the study, still dressed in her T-shirt and jeans, and tried in vain to sleep. Finally, just after five in the morning, she gave up and walked back to the living room. Seth was still at the laptop.

"None of this is your fault," Seth said. "In case that's what was making you toss and turn in there. You've done nothing wrong. You do know that, right?"

Did she? Intellectually she knew she'd done everything by the book and that things would probably have been far worse if she hadn't come to Kilpatrick. But that didn't stop the ache in her chest.

Seth turned back to the screen and the sound of his fingers moving on the keys started up again. "Besides, Travis knew the risks when he formed emotional connections."

Was that fair? Yes, he'd know all the restrictions and conditions of life in Witness Protection. But that didn't mean his heart had been able to stop itself from caring about those little children. Any more than her heart had been able to stop caring about him.

The sound of typing stopped suddenly.

"Jess? We got a problem." Seth's face was ashen in the pale glow of the laptop screen. "Someone is fishing for information about you on the dark web."

Fear poured cold over her shoulders.

"Who?" she asked.

"I don't know yet," Seth said. "It's bouncing off servers and IP addresses, masking sites all over the world. I'm barely able to identify the messages before they disappear. They just flash online with a secure reply link and then are taken down again. Then another one blips on another site. I have no way of knowing how many of these there've been and then they're gone. Think of it like online fly-fishing. Dipping the lure in the water and then quickly disappearing."

The shivers ran colder, and Jess found herself wrapping her arms protectively around her.

"And I'm on the end of that lure?" she asked.

"Yup," Seth confirmed. "Your photo, your name, both the undercover last name you gave when we first came to town and your real name, along with the fact you're an RCMP detective."

Help me, Lord.

"I can trace it and find the source." Seth ran his hand through his already disheveled hair. "But it's not an instantaneous process. It could take me hours. A lot of hours. Maybe even a day or more."

"Hey, it's okay," she said and patted his shoulder. "You're doing the best you can. We all are."

"I wish I could do more and faster." Seth rubbed his hands over his face. "You don't get how frustrating it is to be sitting here, watching these things happen, knowing that sometimes you can catch it and sometimes you can't. No one's ever gotten away from me yet. But sometimes it's taken me weeks or even months to find someone. Even for the best hacker, things take time, and we don't have time."

No, they really didn't.

"Message Liam, Mack and Noah to let them know," Jess said. She didn't know if her entire team would still be awake, but time had seemed to have lost all meaning since the data breach. "Maybe they can speed up that helicopter. I'll go tell Travis."

"What do you want me to tell them?" Seth asked.

"Tell them that my identity has been compromised online, my personal identification has been posted on the dark web, and I need to be pulled from all undercover assignments, including the Chimera," Jess said.

It was as simple as that. It was over. No more undercover assignments. She was not going to be the one to see the Chimera's face, get a positive identification and finally get a warrant issued in his name.

It was over. It was done. And now she had to go tell Travis that the last shred of hope they'd had that she'd be able to take down the Chimera was gone. She walked up the stairs, feeling her feet drag with every step.

The children's bedroom door was open a crack. She stood there for a moment and looked in. Travis was lying on the floor between Willow and Dominic, his eyes closed and one hand stretched out, touching each of their beds, like he was trying to protect them against anything that might harm them.

Her heart lurched. There was something both so soft and strong about him. Something that made her wish she could lie down beside him, on the old farmhouse floor, and join him in keeping the children safe. Instead she prayed, feeling something deep and indefinable break inside her chest.

As if sensing her gaze on him, Travis opened his eyes and smiled with that lazy, unguarded grin of someone who'd just woken up from a happy and pleasant dream and hadn't yet remembered that it's not real.

"Hey," Travis whispered. "Give me a second."

She watched as he slowly unfurled and stood. Then he paused and searched her face, as if finally fully waking and seeing her for real. His forehead creased. "What's wrong?"

So very much. Tears filled her eyes and threatened to fall. "We need to talk."

He nodded then slowly brushed a hand over each sleeping child's form in turn, as if in prayer. He turned and followed her out into the hallway, leaving the door open a crack.

"Can we go somewhere?" she asked softly. "Maybe the front porch?"

"I don't want to be that far away from the kids," he

said. "But Patricia's room has a balcony. We can go talk there."

She nodded and followed as he lead the way down the hall and through a door. Patricia's room was large, with an old antique dresser with pictures on it.

"That's Patricia and her husband, Joe," Travis said, pointing to a black-and-white picture of a young couple who didn't look much older than teenagers. Then he pointed to a square, colored picture of the same couple with a young boy. "They were both first-generation Canadians and met at college. That's them again with Geoff, when he was a little boy."

He pointed to colorful glossy pictures of two laughing teenagers.

"And that's Geoff and Amber," he said. "They were high school sweethearts. Joe died two years after they were married."

She glanced at a picture of Geoff, Amber and Travis sitting on a log, with a toddler in Travis's arms she recognized as Willow.

"That was us one Thanksgiving," he said. "Patricia called me her 'found son.' She said there were two types of family in the world. Those you were born into and those that you found."

Travis turned to Jess. Pain brimmed his eyes. Something tightened in her throat as he searched her face. Then he led her through the large double doors and out onto a balcony. The June night sky lay dark blue and fathomless above them, and for a long moment neither of them said anything.

"I have something to tell you," Jess said finally.

"Your cover's been properly blown, right?" he asked.

Travis reached for both of her hands and took them in his.

"Yeah," she said. "Whoever this petty, evil little Shiny Man is, he's been sending out feelers about me all over the dark web and Seth hasn't been able to locate the source yet. But it doesn't matter. It just means it's all over for me. I won't be able to go undercover against the Chimera. I can't risk any undercover missions anymore." Frustrated tears pushed to the corners of her eyes.

Travis squeezed her hands. "Hey," he said softly. "It's going to be okay."

"How?" she asked. "Criminals have destroyed both your life and mine. I'll never be able to risk going undercover again. We failed to stop the Chimera. We failed to stop one Shiny Man before someone murdered him and haven't caught the Shiny Man who grabbed Willow."

"There's always hope," Travis said. "You know that. I was always the cynic and you were the optimist, remember? You believed in me way more than I ever believed in myself."

"I might never see you again," she said. "As long as you're living under a secret identity, it's too risky."

"I know," Travis said. Something choked in his voice. He pulled her hands to his chest and brought her closer to him. "And yeah, the loss of your ability to go undercover ever again is a huge blow. I know how hard that is. But you'll make it through. You still have your team. You'll reshape and rebuild your career in a new way."

"But we won't have each other," she said.

"No." His voice dropped. "We won't."

When she'd come to Kilpatrick, Jess hadn't known why she'd been so focused on seeing Travis and recruiting him. But now she did. She'd missed him. She'd cared about him. And now the thought of losing him again cut deep inside her.

"If we went back in time, five years ago, and I'd asked you out for coffee, would you have gone?" Travis asked.

She nodded. "Yes, I would've."

"What if I'd asked you out for dinner?' he queried. "On an actual romantic date?"

"Definitely," she said.

"And if I'd told you that I'd had feelings for you?"

"I would've told you I had feelings for you, too." Somehow in the sadness of knowing they had so little time together, she felt a fresh courage fill her core. "I would've told you that I admired you, I liked how your mind worked and how dedicated you were to your job. I would've admitted you were the only man I'd ever really liked the idea of having a future with. And that I liked that idea very much."

There was a very faint roar in the distance, like the threat of thunder, only without even the hint of rain. The rumbling grew louder, and she recognized what it was. A helicopter was approaching.

"I wanted a future with you, too," Travis said. Then he stepped back, and his hands dropped from hers. "But if you'd asked me out on a date, I would've said no. I wasn't the man you deserved back then. I wasn't ready for a family or for you. Don't get me wrong, I wanted to be, more than anything. But I think I knew that God had more work to do in my heart before then. And now..." His voice trailed off.

The noise of the helicopter grew louder. She could see it as a small dot of light against the deep blue sky.

And now it was too late, for both of them. But even if they hadn't had the past, and they didn't have the future, at least they had right now. She stepped forward boldly and slid her hands up around his neck. His arms wrapped around her waist and he pulled her into him.

"I wish I'd grown with you," she said. "When you did all that work to become a man you're proud of being, I wish I'd been right there alongside you, watching it happen. So that on the day you felt ready to be with someone, you'd have looked over and seen me there." She swallowed hard. "Travis, I—"

He kissed her before she could finish the sentence.

They stood there holding each other while the helicopter roared and rumbled closer. It wasn't until she felt the wind of the helicopter landing on the lawn that they pulled out of each other's arms. Then, without a word, Travis went back to the children and Jess ran downstairs.

A cold breeze whipped up the stairs toward her, but it wasn't until she reached the living room that she realized why. The front door was open.

Seth's laptop sat on the table. The screen was black with small green text scrolling across it at a pace she'd never seen before, like all the words it contained were pouring themselves out at a dizzying speed. Then suddenly the screen went black.

Her phone buzzed and she glanced at it. The screen was black, except for a single word flashing red on the screen. Run!

And suddenly she realized that Seth had activated his computer's auto destruct and set their phones to wipe themselves clean. Then what had happened to him? Had he been kidnapped? Killed? There's no way Seth would've just run and left them all behind.

"Travis!" she shouted. "We've got hostiles!"

She turned toward the stairs. But it was too late as a large man in black fatigues stepped out from the kitchen with an automatic weapon, blocking her way. She froze and her hands rose as he aimed the weapon between her eyes.

"Detective Jessica Eddington!" The voice was cold, cruel and had a heavy Eastern European accent. "The Chimera would like to see you."

TWELVE

The Chimera's henchman relieved her of her cell phone and gun. He ordered her to place her hands on her head and marched her out the front door, away from the house and down the driveway. Then he made her stand, the barrel of a gun to her back, and face the farmhouse.

She couldn't see his face, but she didn't need to. She knew his type. The Chimera liked to staff his operations with interchangeable and dangerous criminal mercenaries, mostly from Eastern Europe and former Soviet countries. He'd fly them in and out of the country before law enforcement could catch them. She also knew, without a doubt, that unlike Travis, this man holding her and the others storming the farmhouse had never seen the Chimera's face. Even if her team arrived now, in all its glory and might, and rescued them, grounded the helicopter and took the Chimera's henchmen into custody, they'd still be no closer to discovering his true identity and stopping his evil operation.

Lord, I'm so terrified right now, I don't even know

how or what to pray. Show me the way out. Tell me what to do. Please, please save us now.

Instead, all she could do was watch from a distance, helpless as two more masked men marched Seth, Travis and the children from the farmhouse at gunpoint, with Dominic in his safety harness on Travis's chest and Willow in Seth's arms. She prayed, with all her heart, that the children's half-awake and sleepy state, and the comfort of Travis's strength, would keep them from absorbing the fear of what was happening.

In vain, she looked to the sky, searching for hope in the darkness above as it slowly began to turn to gold at the edges of the horizon. She strained her ears, listening hard, hoping against hope for the sound of rescue coming. But all she could hear was the noise of the rotors and the shaking of the leaves. Travis, Seth and the children disappeared into the helicopter. Then she felt the gun at her back as the large, masked man nudged her forward.

Desperation and despair poured over Jess, flooding her emotions so deeply that for a moment she couldn't move or breathe. Whoever the Chimera was, whatever he was up to, and wherever they were being taken, the most dangerous international criminal she knew had now kidnapped two veteran RCMP detectives, who'd been directly involved in taking down his past operation, along with the country's most elite and skilled hacker, who himself had to disappear into Witness Protection. The havoc the Chimera could now wreak and the damage he could now do was incalculable.

Not to mention he also had two vulnerable children in his grasp as leverage.

The gunman jabbed her with the barrel of his weapon. Her chin rose. Whatever happened next, the people she cared about were not going to face it alone. Tears of desperation filled her eyes. She grit her teeth and stumbled forward, praying with every breath. There had to be a way out of this.

Travis's words from the balcony just moments before echoed in her mind. There had to be hope. Even if she didn't see it. *Come on, Jess. Think!* Travis and Seth would fight with their last breath to save the children, escape and stop the Chimera. Liam and the rest of her team would never give up until they were found and rescued. There were only three mercenaries. They weren't outmanned. But they were outgunned, and by killers who wouldn't think twice about taking them down.

But she, Travis and Seth weren't about to put the children in danger.

Jess walked across the lawn. The helicopter grew nearer. The masked criminal pushed her head down as they walked under the rotors. The helicopter had doors on both sides, with two pairs of seats that faced each other in the back and two seats in the front, separated by what looked like a bulletproof divider.

Travis sat with his back to the cockpit, Dominic strapped to his chest and Willow half curled on his lap. There was an armed and masked man to his right. Seth sat alone on the seat facing them, his face pale and seemingly frozen with fear. Yet, as she glanced from one man to the other, the first glimmer of hope brushed her heart.

Neither Travis nor Seth had been handcuffed.

The gunman forced her in and pointed at the seat beside Seth. Then he slammed the door and went around to the front of the cockpit and took the seat beside the pilot. The masked man sitting across from her balanced his weapon on his lap, steadied it with one hand and tapped his earpiece with the other.

"Tell the Chimera we're on our way," he said, speaking in Ukrainian. Thanks to the language training she'd taken when researching the Chimera, she could understand enough to know what he was saying. "We've got the lady detective. She came without resistance… Also four civilian hostages… Scared and compliant. No problems… Two are little children… Ask him if he wants us to keep them all."

Jess's eyes met Travis's. She watched as they widened.

Four civilian hostages.

And like that, her tiny glimmer of hope sparked and flickered into a tiny flame.

They didn't know who they had. They were after her—and only her. As far as they were concerned, Seth, Travis and the kids were expendable. It wasn't much of an advantage. But it was something and she'd take it.

The helicopter began to rise. She gasped a breath, filling her lungs with courage. Then she met Travis's eyes again and prayed silently both for God's help and that Travis would know what to do. He nodded slightly as if reading her mind.

Now all she could do was pray, hope and act.

She spun around on her seat, grabbing for her door handle. But before she could even reach it, the mercenary across from her leaped, shoving her back against the seat hard and grabbing hold of her hands.

"Stop!" he barked in English. "Or I will make this journey very unpleasant!"

Her hands were trapped in his. Her body was pressed back against the seat. And still the helicopter rose. He forced her hands down to her sides. Men swore and shouted to him from the front seat in a mixture of Russian dialects and he shouted back. The barrel of his weapon slipped to the side as he fished a zip tie from his pocket and looped it around her thin wrists to fasten them together. As he did, Jess struck out. Using the man's pressure on her wrists as an anchor, she spun her body around at lightning speed, raised both legs and glanced at Seth.

"Stay safe!" she shouted and kicked the hacker hard with both legs, propelling Seth backward off the seat and against the far door, just as Travis leaned over and opened it for him. Seth's eyes widened and prayer escaped his lips as he fell, tumbling out of the helicopter and onto the ground just ten feet below.

Thank You, God.

"We have to land!" the man holding her shouted.

Wind whipped at them through the open door. The helicopter swayed unsteadily. The mercenary slapped Jess hard across the face, knocking her head back against the seat. She felt the zip tie yanked hard around

her wrists and pain shot through her arms as he teth-
ered her to the seat.

She kicked back hard at her kidnapper, trying to
knock his high-powered rifle away from him before he
could fully regain his grip on it. Yet, as she fought and
thrashed, she watched as Travis brushed a kiss across
the top of Willow's head, scooped her up into his arms
and slid her toward the door.

"Be brave and trust Seth," he said. "He'll catch you."

The helicopter rose. Eighteen feet. Twenty feet. Willow jumped. Her tiny body tumbled through the air.
Jess's heart froze. Then she watched through the open
door as Seth caught the little girl in his arms.

Seth hugged Willow tightly to his chest and ran
with her toward the farmhouse. Prayers of thanksgiving swelled in Jess's heart. The helicopter dropped suddenly, taking her stomach with it. She looked out. They
were back to hovering just twelve feet off the ground.

"We have to get back!" the mercenary yelled.

"No!" another masked man shouted. "Let them go!
We just need her."

A truck, red and battered, raced down the driveway
toward the farmhouse. The window rolled down and
Nick Henry, Liam's military friend, leaned out. He fired
a handgun at the rising helicopter. The mercenary in the
front seat returned fire and the truck windshield shattered. Her captor regained his weapon and aimed it at
Jess, his colleagues screaming orders in his headset.
But Travis leaped to his feet and, with a strong blow,
knocked the man sideways. The mercenary slumped
back against the seat, momentarily stunned as the he-

licopter lurched upward. She looked at Travis, where he now crouched with the open door behind him and Dominic still in the harness on his chest.

"Go!" she shouted. "Now! Save Dominic while you still can! I'll be okay."

Somehow. In some way. She had to have faith.

Pain flooded the depths of Travis's eyes. "Not without you!"

"You have to!"

He had to let her go. Couldn't he see this was the only way?

The mercenary stumbled to his feet.

Travis's eyes met hers.

"I will find you," he said. "I promise."

Then he leapt from the helicopter.

Travis fell through the air, wrapping his arms protectively around the baby on his chest and cradling him with his arms. Wind rushed past. The ground came up toward them. He lowered his head over Dominic's and curled his body around the little boy's body as he stretched one arm out to take the blow.

He hit the ground and rolled, tumbling over in the grass and shielding Dominic with his body. Then he leaped to his feet and ran for the safety of the farmhouse. He reached the porch and looked back. The helicopter was rising. One of the Chimera's mercenary was leaning out the open door, ineffectually showering the ground with bullets. Travis pressed against the wall and felt his heart tear in his chest as he watched the helicopter disappear over the horizon, taking Jess with it.

Lord, please keep her safe and help me find her.

Then he looked down. Dominic blinked up at him, his eyes wide with shock. Travis slid down and sat back against the wall, removing Dominic from his carrier and checking him for injury. Dominic giggled. Travis thanked God and brushed a kiss over the top of the baby's head. The baby squealed happily and reached out his arms as Willow and Seth ran toward them.

"Dominic!" Willow shouted. And Travis was barely able to open his arms before Willow launched into them. Travis hugged them both tightly, for one long moment. Then his eyes rose to the helicopter as it disappeared in the distance. It was gone. And so was Jess.

"Don't worry." Seth's voice was by his side. "We'll get her back."

"How?" Travis asked. He hadn't meant to say the word out loud, but now there it was. "How do we get her back?"

"I don't know yet," Seth admitted. "All the tools I had at the house have been destroyed. I've got no way of tracking the helicopter."

"Find a way," Travis said. "Figure it out. If anyone can, it's you."

He glanced at Nick, coming up across the lawn behind them. Without a word, Nick handed Seth a cell phone and Seth immediately started typing.

And I just have to trust Jess's team to do their job, Travis thought. Then he prayed. *I feel helpless right now, Lord. Just like I was when I came to Kilpatrick.*

Travis rose slowly, helping Willow to her feet and sliding Dominic into the crook of his arm as he did so.

"Please tell me you have emergency medical training," Travis said.

Nick nodded. "Enough to check the kids and make sure they're okay."

"Thank you," Travis said, "again. For this. For everything."

"No problem." Nick nodded. "I'm just glad I could help. Liam called me as soon as you went silent. Gotta admit, I didn't expect to get fired at by a helicopter." He glanced back at his truck. It was riddled with bullet holes and the front windshield was destroyed.

"Looks like Liam owes you a truck," Seth quipped.

"I owe him a motorcycle," Nick said. "As well as eternal gratitude for helping me save the life of my wife and child." He ran his hand over his face as if a memory had crossed his mind. "If it wasn't for his help at a crucial time, I might have lost them both. He also helped solve my sister's murder."

"I'd like to hear the story one day," Travis said, "when the dust settles."

And Jess was back beside him.

Seth's furious typing turned into a phone call that Travis couldn't hear either side of. Dominic wriggled from Travis's hands. He set him down on the porch, but Dominic grabbed Travis's leg and pulled himself up to standing.

"Do you have a son or daughter?" Travis asked.

"One of each," Nick said. "Zander turns seven this year, and Rosie is one."

What must this man think of him? He'd jumped from

a helicopter holding Dominic. He'd told Willow to jump. And he'd lost Jess to kidnappers.

"Ever feel they deserve better?" Travis asked.

"Every single day." Nick chuckled. "I figure every good father and husband does. Every wife, mother and caregiver, too."

"Okay," Seth said. "So here's the good news. If I take my laptop to the bookstore, I can use the rudimentary framework I created when I upgraded your security system to access the remote backup I created of my computer when I wiped all my devices clean. Then we're back in business and I can launch a wide sweep for Jess. Liam is now scrambling to change our evacuation plan. He'll give you an hour to pack up anything you need."

Right, because once they left, they were never coming back.

They said goodbye to Nick and went back into the house just long enough to get the kids dressed and fed, and to pack a few things. Then Travis said goodbye to the house that had been like a home to him.

The sun was rising as they reached the bookstore. To his surprise the door was open, and the store was packed. His volunteer firefighter crew, local business owners, members of his church and parents from Willow's school were working together to stack books, tidy shelves and sweep. Hot coffee and fresh pastries were being served by Harris, Cleo and Alvin on the shiny-clean snack bar.

A cheer arose as they entered the store. Person after person came up, patted him on the shoulder and hugged him before moving back to work. Willow ran over to join a group of her friends and their parents on the carpet and Travis set a wriggling Dominic down beside her.

Something in his heart swelled. He'd just been planning on just sneaking out of town and slipping off without saying goodbye to anyone. And now, without knowing it, the town had come together and showed up giving him one more last chance to see them all.

"This town really loves Patricia and those kids." The gruff voice came from his left. He turned. Chief Gordon Peters was standing just to the side of the door, in full uniform, his chest puffed up in that usual pose, like he was about to take a deep breath.

"Yeah, they really do," Travis said.

"I'm sorry we haven't found a lead yet on who tried to grab Willow at the Spring Concert yesterday," the police chief added. "But we won't give up until we figure out who it was."

"Thank you," Travis said.

"You know, you could've told me that your ex-lady was a cop," Chief Peters said. He snorted. "Might explain something about why she left you."

Something bristled at the back of Travis's neck. He'd held his tongue for far too long. Maybe Travis-of-Kilpatrick didn't have the same bite that Travis-the-detective had. But that was before he'd seen the woman he cared about snatched by evil men.

Travis crossed his arms. "What's your problem with me? Why don't you like me?" Travis asked.

The chief blinked. "I assure you I—"

"Don't!" Travis cut him off. "Please. Just be blunt with me. You've never liked me, and you've always made snide comments about my file. So right now, man to man, tell me why."

Chief Peters crossed his arms, matching Travis's stance, and something hardened behind his eyes.

"I don't like reckless drivers," he said. "You should get that, after what happened to Geoff and Amber. You were in my town less than two weeks before you crash into a tree and, according to your file, you're a repeat offender when it comes to breaking speed limits and driving recklessly. I lost a very close buddy that way once, when another driver fell asleep and plowed into him. And I've worked way too many accident scenes. I've got no patience for people like you."

Well, then.

"Fair enough," Travis said. "But people change. I did. Patricia might never recover and the kids might need the community's help." *Especially once I leave their lives and they need a foster family.* "So I hope you meant it when you said you'd be there for them, regardless of what you think of me."

The chief blew out a hard breath and didn't answer. Travis watched as Willow scampered around the room with her friends, picking up fallen books as she went. As she ran past Alvin, the kindergarten teaching scooped her up into his arms, hugging her from behind, and whispered something in her ear.

"No!" Willow shouted. "No, you can't buy my fav'rite book! Not for lotsa moneys!"

The room faded away from Travis's eyes as he watched Willow whimper and try to pull from Alvin's grasp. He knew, without a doubt, that Willow was terrified.

"Alvin!" Travis shouted. "Let her go!"

The kindergarten teacher laughed. A loud, disarming chuckle, with a grin full of teeth. "Hey, she's fine, aren't you, Willow?" Alvin chuckled and let her go with a little pat on the back. "She's fine. I just made a joke and she's just being silly."

Willow ran across the room toward Travis. She wrapped her arms around his leg and he brushed a hand over her head.

He looked down at her. "Is everything okay?"

Willow shook her head. Her voice rose. "He's the Shiny Man who ki'napped me."

Travis locked eyes on Seth's across the room and nodded at him to pick up Dominic. He felt facts click rapid-fire through his mind. Alvin needed money for his master's degree. He'd had the opportunity to grab Willow. He'd have known about Braden from Cleo.

And Willow was certain it was him.

"I'm so sorry, chief," he said. In a single, swift move, he yanked the cop's weapon out of his holster, moved Willow behind him protectively and aimed the gun at Alvin. "Where is Jess?"

THIRTEEN

The room froze. Travis held the weapon steady and aimed it between the kindergarten teacher's eyes.

"Travis." A warning rumbled through Chief Peters voice. "Give me back my weapon."

"I wish I could," Travis said. "But Alvin is the Shiny Man who tried to kidnap Willow yesterday. He gave information about Jess online to some really bad criminals who've kidnapped her, and I'd do anything to get her back."

Alvin laughed. "What is this? Some kind of joke?"

"Slide your cell phone across the floor to Seth," Travis said. "Then put your hands on your head and get down."

Something went cold in Alvin's eyes that belied the artificially wide grin on his face. His hand twitched down to a faint lump at the side of his sweatshirt.

"Stop!" Travis ordered. "You so much as try to reach for that gun and I'll shoot!"

Voices babbled around the room. There were a million different ways this could go wrong. And only one way he could make it go right.

"I'm a former undercover detective with the RCMP," Travis said. "I've wanted to tell all of you that, so many times. But I've been in witness protection for the past four years, after taking down a particularly nasty international crime lord's operation with the help of my partner, Jess."

Eyes blinked and jaws dropped. But legs and arms still tensed as if to strike.

"And yeah—" he glanced at Chief Peters "—I was a selfish driver and not the greatest man. But Jess is an incredible RCMP detective, the best person I've ever met, and, thanks to Alvin, is now in the hands of a major crime lord. All that matters now is saving her."

The kindergarten teacher smirked, but the look in his eyes grew colder.

"And why would I do any of that?" Alvin asked.

"I don't know yet," Travis admitted. "But I'll figure it out." For now, he'd focus on how. Then he glanced at Cleo, huddling with her dad behind the counter. "If I'm right, then Alvin and Braden were working together. He betrayed your trust, teamed up with your abusive ex and used you as an alibi. That means Alvin called Braden for updates and to give him direction while you were at the hospital with Patricia. Is that possible? Did he make secret phone calls while you were together? Calls he didn't let you overhear?"

"Don't answer that!" Alvin snapped.

But it was too late. Cleo had already nodded. "He did."

One step closer. Thank You, God.

"You all know me," Travis said, glancing around

the room. "You've prayed with me, had meals with me, and played baseball with me. I've helped put out your fires—both real and metaphorical—and you've helped put out mine. Right now, I need your help to save Jess."

A pause spread through the room, filling the store and spreading between the books.

"Son," Chief Peters said, his voice firm and strong, "give me back my gun."

"Look, I know it sounds crazy," Travis said. "But all I need is his cell phone. It'll take my buddy Seth here a couple of minutes to prove if what I'm saying is right. If I'm wrong, you can arrest me and I'll go without argument. If I'm right, Jess's life is on the line."

"Come on!" Alvin said. "You can't believe him!"

"Detective!" Chief Peters's voice rose. "Stop dillydallying, hand me back my weapon and go get his phone."

Travis took a deep breath, prayed for wisdom and handed Chief Peters the gun.

"Thank you." The chief turned the weapon on the kindergarten teacher. "Give him the phone, Alvin." Then he glanced around the room. "Show's over. Everyone get out of here. Quickly and safely. Go."

People began to evacuate along the sides of the room as the cop turned to his shoulder mic and called for backup. Travis realized suddenly that Chief Peters could've called for backup at any time before, instead of hearing him out.

Travis started across the floor toward Alvin. But before he'd gotten halfway across the room, Alvin's hand darted to his side. The kindergarten teacher yanked out a gun and pointed it at Travis.

"Just let me go and nobody gets hurt!" Alvin shouted.

Travis rolled his eyes and leaped, feeling years of dormant instincts course through his body as he caught Alvin around the middle, forcing the gun over his head as he brought him to the ground. He pressed Alvin back against the floor hard with one hand. With the other, he pried the weapon from his hand and sent it sliding across the floor to Chief Peters.

Alvin looked up at him, his eyes wide and manic. "Okay, you're right. But I can tell you how to reach the Chimera. I can give you the dark web IP addresses he used to contact me. I'll tell you everything you need to know. All I want is ten thousand dollars cash and that brat's weird, upside-down picture book."

Willow's favorite bedtime storybook? That's what all this was about?

"I'm not negotiating." Travis pinned him down.

"You can't search my phone without a warrant!" Alvin snarled. "You need me to give you the password, otherwise by the time you get a warrant to crack my phone, Jess will be dead."

"Oh, I'm a former detective," Travis said. "Seth's not law enforcement at all. And if Chief Peters wants to arrest me for snooping through someone's phone, I will gladly plead guilty and take the misdemeanor."

He yanked the phone from Alvin's sweatshirt pocket and slid it across the floor to Seth.

"Crack it," Travis said. "Find the Chimera. Tell him that the RCMP detective who took down his operation, saw his face and missed the shot is very much alive and wants to trade his own life for Detective Jessica Eddington's."

The helicopter was turning around. Jess could feel it moving beneath her, but all she could see out the windows was an endless field of sky. She didn't know how long she'd been sitting in the back of a helicopter with a gun pointed at her face and her hands tied together. But all that time she'd been flying, not knowing where she was going or what awaited her, she'd had something important to hold on to—the others had escaped. Willow and Dominic had been rescued. Seth was okay, would contact her team and they'd mount a rescue.

Travis would find her. She didn't know how or when, but somehow she had faith that she would see him again. Her former partner, the one who'd always tugged at her heartstrings, the man she liked, respected and admired most in the world somehow had feelings for her. Just like she did for him.

The helicopter began to dip. They sank, lower and lower, until she felt the jolt of ground beneath her as they landed.

She looked out the window. They were in a small airfield surrounded by trees. Were they still in Ontario? Were they in northern Manitoba or southern Nunavut? Had they somehow crossed into the United States? A large black and windowless van was parked on the tarmac. She'd seen enough nearly identical vehicles in photos and case files to know that when someone took an unwilling and non-optional ride in one, they usually didn't come back.

The helicopter door in front of her was opened by one masked man in dark fatigues, while another slit her zip-tied hands free from the seat, yanked her arms together, retied her wrists and then practically shoved her so hard she nearly fell.

These was all scare tactics. Ones that she and Travis had studied all too well. It was all intended to frighten and intimidate people into complying and to keep them from trying to escape. Her jaw clenched as she made her way across the tarmac toward the waiting van. Knowing with every step that no matter what they did to cow her, it wouldn't work. No matter what, she would never give up hope.

She was shoved into the back of the van. It was partitioned just like the helicopter, with a wall of what looked like bulletproof glass separating the front seats from the back and a screen mounted behind the driver. She fell onto one of the two bench seats that ran across the van lengthwise and sat awkwardly without a seat belt. Two masked men climbed into the back with her, then two others got into the front and they drove off.

Her captors were talking both to each other and on their phones in a mixture of Ukrainian and Russian, their words clipped and static. She leaned her head against the wall of the vehicle and closed her eyes, pretending not to listen in or to understand the snatches of words and conversation as they moved around her.

"...GPS coordinates..."

"...he's a high-risk individual..."

"...Chimera will want visual confirmation..."

The texture of the ground changed beneath the tires of the vehicle as the van slowed. She could hear the faint sound of rushing water fill her ears as the back door of the van sprang open.

She opened her eyes and then she saw him.

Travis.

Her former partner was standing alone, without any obvious backup, vehicle or weapon, on a long bridge that arched high over what sounded like a river.

Improbably, and despite all obstacles, her brave, stubborn, impossible and incredible man had found her. One of the masked men bounded out of the back and shouted at Travis to raise his hands and approach the van.

Travis turned, stretched his strong arms up to the sky, and walked slowly toward them. His chin was raised and his eyes were strong. When he got about twelve feet away, a second masked man jumped out from the passenger-side door and told Travis to drop to his knees and place his hands on his head. He did so.

One man kept a gun trained on Travis, while the other patted him down, confiscated his cell phone and smashed it on the ground under his feet. Then he slowly waved a metal detector over Travis for good measure, making sure he had no weapons of any kind. And all the while, Travis's gaze never left Jess's face. He was ordered back to his feet, his hands were zip-tied in front of him and then he was shoved toward the door and onto the bench seat across from Jess. Travis's eyes met hers, and although neither of them spoke, she could feel the weight of unspoken words move through the silence between them.

One masked man shut the door and then went around and got in the front of the van. The other touched the screen mounted behind the driver's seat. It flickered to life and the featureless silhouette of a man's face appeared, an indistinct part of a city skyline behind him.

Even before she heard his distorted voice, she knew it was the Chimera.

"Yeah," the Chimera said. "That's the guy. How you were stupid enough to have him in your grasp earlier and let him get away will be dealt with later. In the meantime, bring them both to me."

"Wait!" Travis's voice rose high and like a shout. "Mr. Chimera, sir! You promised me you'd let her go, if I turned myself in. That was the deal!"

The Chimera didn't respond. He just laughed. It was a low, guttural, dismissive sound. Then he ended the video call.

The vehicle started to rumble across the bridge. Travis leaped to his feet, in a single swift motion, before their captors could even respond. His hands clenched and arms flexed as he raised them above his head and brought them down so sharply the zip ties snapped.

The mercenaries' weapons swung toward him.

"Jess!" he shouted. "Close your eyes! Now!"

FOURTEEN

Jess shut her eyes tightly. The light that filled the van was so bright, sharp and blinding that even with her eyes closed she could see the world lighten beneath her eyelids. Voices shouted. The van spun wildly, careening out of control. Then she felt Travis launching himself at her, wrapping his arms around her and pulling her tight into his chest.

"Hang on!" Travis shouted. "It's going to get rough."

But even as he said the words, she heard the loud, screeching sound of metal smashing against metal. The van jolted hard, tossing them sideways. The masked men's shouting and swearing grew louder. They were panicking, their eyes hurting, and she remembered what being hit by that light for the first time had been like, before she'd known it was temporary. Then she felt the world drop out from underneath them as the van flew off the edge of the bridge and down toward the raging river below.

They struck the water nose-first. The van began to sink.

"Now to get out of here," Travis said.

She opened her eyes. They were sideways, halfway up the back of the sinking van, their feet braced against the end of the bench. She glanced down to see the two masked men, flailing and disoriented, as their eyesight began to recover. Travis reached up and shoved the van's back door open. Pale blue sky lay ahead. Sunlight filled her eyes.

"Come on." Travis wrapped one arm around her waist. With the other he reached up and grabbed the edge of the open door. "You can still swim, right?"

"I can kick," she said, "but my hands are tied."

"It's okay, I'll help you."

They pushed off against the seat and Travis shoved his way out of the sinking van, lifting her along with him and leaving the masked men behind as they scrambled for their weapons.

Travis and Jess half jumped and half fell into the water. The river rushed cold and hard around them, threatening to pull them under. But Travis's arm stayed tight around her waist as he swam with her toward the shore. She felt the ground under her feet as they stumbled together out of the river and toward the muddy slope. The sound of motors seemed to rumble from all sides, growing louder by the moment. She looked around and counted three RCMP rescue boats coming at them rapid-speed down the river and saw two police helicopters cresting the horizon.

Her head shook in amazement. "How did you do all this?"

"It was your team," he said. "They're pretty amazing. I probably should've listened to you all a lot sooner."

Travis helped her up the slope and away from the water's edge. He didn't stop until they reached the top of the bank and were back on the bridge. There was a gaping hole of twisted railing metal where the van had broken through. She looked down. The van still bobbed in the water, and it looked like all of the masked mercenaries had made it out and were swimming to shore, only to be greeted by armed officers. A sigh of relief left her lungs.

Travis slid his hands down her arms and onto her bound wrists. He cradled her fingers in one of his hands.

"Hang on," he said. "I have something for that."

He pulled what looked like a tiny ceramic blade from deep within his pocket, slid it between the zip ties and sliced through. Her arms fell free. She threw them around his neck and he pulled her close.

"How did…?" Her words faltered on her lips as she looked into his deep and fathomless eyes.

"How did I break my own zip ties?" he asked. "A combination of knowing when and how to flex my muscles when they slipped them on me, and some skill in ripping my hands apart. Like I said, I had a lot of free time when I moved here and watched a lot of online videos."

She laughed and felt him pull her closer.

"I meant how did all of this happen?" she asked. "How did you find me? How did you use a tactical light against them? How did you summon the cavalry?"

"Willow found the Shiny Man," he said. "It was her teacher, Alvin Walker. There was a cleanup effort at the bookstore this morning and when Alvin put his arms around Willow, she knew it was him instantly. Chief Peters then stepped in to arrest him.

"For some reason he badly wanted to get his hands on her special bedtime storybook. Hopefully, Seth can research it and tell us why. Alvin was coordinating with Braden when he and Cleo took Patricia to the hospital. Seth got hold of Alvin's phone, used it to track down the Chimera, and put out the word I was willing to trade my life for yours."

Another RCMP helicopter roared over them, drowning out Travis's voice. They waited while it passed.

"Liam managed the RCMP side of the operation," Travis said, "including securing the rendezvous spot. Seth used the Shiny Man's goodies to rig an explosive light that would pass a metal detector, in case the Chimera's men scanned me for weapons. Seth is back in Kilpatrick with the kids, coordinating the tech side. He used a cell signal pinging device hidden in the smashed phone to track the Chimera's signal and triangulate his location. As soon as he gets a location, several RCMP teams are standing by in major city centers to swoop in and take them down. I'm just thankful your team trusted me to be the one to go in and rescue you."

"You told the Chimera that you were there to trade your life for mine," she said.

"If all else had failed," Travis said, "I would've. One hundred percent. Surely, you know I'd do anything for you."

"I do," she said, "and you know I would for you."

A grin turned at the corners of his generous mouth.

He brushed his fingers along the line of her jaw. He lowered his face toward hers. Their lips met.

"Jess!" Liam's voice boomed to her right. "Travis!"

They pulled back. Her colleague and friend was pelting down the bridge toward them. The large man paused and glanced at each of them in turn, like he wasn't sure how to interpret the moment he'd barged into. "We've got to go. Patricia Tatlow has woken up!"

An RCMP helicopter flew them straight to Sudbury. Seth and the children were already en route in a different chopper and would meet them there.

Travis and Jess sat side by side in the back, with their fingers linked. He hadn't let go of Jess's hand once since they'd fastened their seat belts, and she hadn't let go of his, either. He had no idea what would happen next. All he knew was that he never wanted to let go of her hand again.

"The RCMP division in Victoria, British Columbia, has made an arrest," Liam said. He leaned toward them and handed Travis a tablet computer. "Hopefully it's the Chimera. We need you to make a positive identification."

Travis glanced at the screen. The face of a stranger with a strong jaw and firm eyes stared back at him. His heart sank. It wasn't him. *Lord, whoever the Chimera is and wherever he's disappeared to, please may he be caught one day.* Travis shook his head and handed the tablet back.

"No, I'm sorry," Travis said. "Whoever that man is, he's not the Chimera."

"Good," Liam said with a chuckle. "That's my buddy Jacob. If he was the Chimera, we'd have a big problem. Just had to make sure you weren't eager to finger the first face you saw." He flicked the screen and two more faces came up. "How about these?"

More strangers. "No." Travis shook his head.

Liam nodded and pulled up two more faces. Travis glanced at the screen. This time he didn't hesitate for a moment.

"This one." He pointed to the face on the left. "This man's the Chimera."

"You sure?" Liam's eyebrow rose.

"Absolutely," Travis said. "No two ways about it."

Liam let out a long sigh of relief and leaned back against the seat. Then he grabbed his phone and dialed a number. "Hey, it's me. Witness was presented with five photos and identified Alexi Viktor, the man we have in custody." He grit his teeth as he grinned. "Looks like we finally got him."

Travis could almost feel the palpable relief that swept over Jess. But Travis felt oddly cold, as he stared down at the man's face on his screen. He'd only gotten a glimpse of the man before, but now that he could really study his face, he was struck by how bland it was in its ordinariness.

Alexi Viktor, aka the Chimera, was slightly overweight and slightly bald. He had the kind of pale skin that implied he spent most of his life behind a desk and an everyday unattractiveness that made him the kind of person who'd be overlooked and ignored, instead of stared at. It was an incredibly unremarkable ordinariness that had made it so hard for anyone to match the police sketch Travis had provided and thus allowed the Chimera to pass through so many international airports without being noticed.

But there was something else in the face, too. The slight sneer at the corner of his mouth and a glint of arrogance in his eyes that showed he thought whoever the person was who'd snapped his picture during his arrest was so far beneath him they didn't even count as human. Yeah, Travis had seen that look in the Chimera's eyes first-hand when he'd missed his shot. He'd never forget it.

He leaned back against the seat as finally the tension he'd been carrying fell from his shoulders.

Thank you, Lord. Just...thank you.

"There's been a huge sweep of his entire place," Liam said. "It's the same holiday complex that Jess was scheduled to work at. Over four dozen people were arrested. We also rescued several others who claimed they'd being forced to work there against their will."

Liam stretched like he hadn't slept in days.

"As for the second case you were working, that's been wrapped up, too," Liam said. "Looks like Alvin Walker was indeed the man who tipped off the Chimera to where you were, but that's the only connection between the two cases. Alvin has confessed to being the man behind the Shiny Man persona, after police found respirator masks, construction jumpsuits and chloroform in his car and apartment. Alvin had contacted Braden after hearing Cleo talk about him, figuring he needed a criminal to do the dirty work and give him an alibi. They both wore the masks at different times. Alvin claimed he accidentally killed Braden in an argument."

"After sedating him with chloroform," Travis said and shook his head, "and before hanging him in the living room of an abandoned house. I suspect the timing of his crimes is down to the time of year. Just like the Chimera was gearing up his operation for the summer, Alvin was facing down the end of the school year before summer vacation. I would not be surprised if he wasn't going to be returning to school in September, for whatever reason. Plus he was accepted to a master's degree program at Queen's."

"You'd be right about that," Liam affirmed. He glanced at Jess, like they were sharing an inside joke Travis didn't understand. "Apparently the school principal had warned him he'd probably be laid off over the summer when the government announced education budget cuts. That would mean moving back home with his parents in Guelph or taking a job elsewhere."

"So it was now or never," Travis said.

Liam nodded. "We still don't have a motive. Any thoughts on that?"

"Of course we do," Travis said. "He wanted Willow's picture book. I'm guessing it's valuable."

A wry smile curled at the corner of Liam's lips. He glanced at Jess. "You were right about him."

She laughed. "Of course I was."

"Are you sure you don't want to get back into police work?" he asked Travis. "Because the ability to close two mostly unrelated cases in less than forty-eight hours, while also dealing with major personal issues, is the kind of thing we look for in a cop."

"I'm sure." Travis glanced at Jess and, for one long moment, was lost anew in the endless blue of her eyes. Then he felt her head drop gently against his shoulder. "I'm not saying I'll never help out on a case again. I like your team and you can count me in if you ever need me. I just don't want to ever wear a badge again, go back to the life I had, or be the man I was."

The helicopter touched down on the roof of the hospital. They got out and made their way through the door, down the staircase and along the hallway, until he saw Seth standing outside a hospital room.

"I hear we got our man, both of them," Seth said. Hope tinged the hacker's tired smile. "The kids are in there."

Travis stopped and looked through the window, feeling Jess gently pull her hand from his.

Patricia lay propped up on the hospital bed. Willow sat in a chair next to the bed, her head resting beside her Nan while Patricia ran her hand over the little girl's head. Her other hand brushed Dominic's tiny fingers, as a nurse held him by Patricia's bedside.

Travis waited a long moment as she delighted over her grandchildren. Then the nurse led Willow and Dominic out, and waved that he could come in.

Travis glanced at Jess. "Come with me. I want her to meet you."

"No, you go," she said quietly. She squeezed his hand. "You need to have an important conversation and I'll be right here, waiting for you when you get back."

He let go of her hand, slipped inside the hospital room and crossed the floor toward Patricia's bed.

"Hey, Patricia," he said softly. He dropped into a chair. Her face was pale and her skin seemed more translucent and fragile than ever, but her smile was one of the brightest he'd ever seen. "How are you feeling?"

The words seemed so inadequate for the situation, but for now they were the only ones he had.

"Alive," Patricia said. "Also blessed and thankful. The doctor thinks I have a little while longer on this earth. Might be months. Might even be a year. But I'll take whatever the Lord gives me." The smile on her lips echoed in her eyes. "Did you think about my question? Will you raise my grandkids for me when I'm gone?"

How could she still ask him that? Had no one filled her in? Hadn't she heard about what had happened in the past few days?

"Patricia," he said. "I'm a cop. At least, I was. I was a detective with the RCMP for over a decade, taking down some pretty terrible people. I didn't randomly move to Kilpatrick. I was placed there by Witness Protection. And see that woman outside the window?" He glanced at Jess. "She was my RCMP partner."

Patricia let out a long breath.

His chest ached. "I'm so sorry, I wish I'd told you sooner," he said. "But I couldn't. I love Willow and Dominic more than anything and I'll do everything in my power to protect them. But I'm not the man you think I am."

"It's okay." She patted his hand. "On some level, I always knew you were a cop. Not officially. But it showed in the way you talked about people and looked out for them. You were like Joe, Geoff and Amber, and that's why we were so drawn to you, like you were one of us. Are you going to go back to being a cop?"

"No." He shook his head. "Or if so, not the way I was. I might help on cases. What I'd like is to help raise the kids and run the bookstore."

"Then I'll draw up the paperwork and make you their father," Patricia said. "Just promise you'll surround the kids with a lot of family who love them and who'll help raise them."

He thought of Seth and the crowd of people who'd showed up at the bookstore. "I will, I promise."

"And the woman you care about, she'll help love the kids, too?" Patricia asked.

Oh, he had no doubt in his mind that Jess would be an amazing mother to Willow and Dominic, and an incredible wife, but...

"I haven't asked her to be with me," he said.

Patricia laughed softly. "Then what are you waiting for?"

"I don't know," he admitted.

Because as he turned and looked through the window at the beautiful woman standing in the hospital hallway, he felt like he'd been waiting a lifetime for her already.

"One minute," he said. He noticed Patricia was smiling as he left the hospital room.

Jess's head rose. Travis took Jess's hand without a word and lead her down the hall, until he found an empty room, with table and chairs and a large picture window overlooking the endless trees beyond.

"How'd she take it?" Jess asked.

"Well," Travis said. "She still wants me to adopt the kids."

Even as he spoke the words, he still felt stunned. Willow and Dominic were going to be his children?

"Patricia loves you," Jess said. "When you love someone, you accept all the sides of them, even the hard ones."

He looked down at Jess's hand linked through his. Had he really found a woman who was able to accept all the sides of him? Was he ready to step up and be the man she needed him to be?

"I need to tell you something," she added.

He swallowed hard. "I need to ask you something first."

And yet, as he felt the words forming on his lips, she squeezed his hand tightly and spoke his name.

"Travis… Don't… Not now…"

And somehow he knew that she needed him to stop talking.

He pressed his lips together and nodded, even while he felt his own heart urging him to speak.

"Liam's found a new witness protection solution for you, Patricia and the kids," Jess said. The sinking feeling inside his chest seemed to mirror the weight he could see in her eyes. "It's going to take some time to access when it will be safe for you all to return to Kilpatrick. Could be weeks. Could be months."

Could even be years, Travis thought.

"He's found you a cottage that's part of a summer camp about an hour north of here," Jess went on. "It's a really nice place. There will be onsite nursing and medical staff to take care of Patricia, in a hospice situation. There's a helicopter pad, so she can be flown there by air ambulance whenever she's ready to be moved. There's a lake and swimming for the kids, along with daycare for Dominic and summer programs Willow can take part in. As far as Willow will know, she's at camp with her family for the summer. If the situation stretches into September, there's a good school nearby. Most important, it's off the grid and you'll have around-the-clock protection."

"It sounds perfect," he said. Except something about the way her lips curved down at the edges told him that it wouldn't be, because she wouldn't be there. "What about you?"

"I have to go back to work," she said. "There's a lot to be done now that the Chimera's been arrested, and I'm an expert on the case. Once that's wrapped up, I have a whole stack of other very important cases on my desk to get to. There are people in trouble who're counting on cops like me to help, protect and rescue them. As much as I'd love to just spend my summer hanging out with you and the kids at the lakeside, but I just put my job on hold…"

Her words faded on her lips as her eyes look down to his hand holding hers. Then her eyes looked back up at his face and somehow he knew, without being told, she'd have followed him anywhere if only she'd been able to find a way. He wanted to tell her he loved her. He wanted to confess how much he'd missed her and ask her to stay by his side and never leave again.

Instead, words failed him as he opened his mouth and all he could do was nod.

For a long moment, neither of them said anything.

"This is the right outcome," Jess said. "We've wrapped up two cases in three days. We stopped criminals and we saved lives. We've always known that, regardless of anything else that we felt for each other, it was always going to end this way."

But what did this mean for his heart and hers? Would he ever see her again?

Before he could find his voice, she stood on her tip-toes and brushed her lips across his. He kissed her back, briefly and sweetly.

"I love you," he whispered.

"I love you, too."

She rested her head against his chest, he wrapped his arms around her and held her there for one long moment. Then she pulled out of his arms and walked back out into the hallway. And he knew, no matter how many professional conversations they had in the next few hours or days as she helped them all relocate before she left, that this would always be their real goodbye.

FIFTEEN

Mid-July sun flitted over the lake, sending golden light dancing on the deep blue waters. Travis stood on the edge of the wooden dock, rolled a flat stone around in his fingers and then sent it skipping across the water. It bounced seven times before finally sinking and disappearing beneath the depths. His heart knew the feeling. He glanced back at the blissful scene behind him.

The children—soon to be his son and his daughter, by the grace of God—sat on the small strip of beach by the water's edge happily piling sand into either small castles or large mud pies, Travis wasn't quite sure. Willow seemed to have grown an entire inch since school ended, while Dominic had been so excited to figure out how to stand and toddle, that Travis had to baby-proof every inch of space in the cottage. He imagined the little boy would be running by Thanksgiving.

Patricia was curled up in a chair on the porch, reading lazily while she watched the children, the hospice nurse that witness protection had provided sitting beside her. The doctor's last update had been hopeful that Patricia might make it to Christmas, although this might be her last summer.

His eyes rose to the pale blue sky above, dotted with the small, puffy white clouds that he and Willow had been finding animal shapes in all summer.

Lord, You've blessed me beyond my wildest dreams and given me so much more than I deserve. I'm so grateful.

And yet, with every piece of good news, every moment of joy and every unexpected gift God had given him in the past two weeks, Travis hadn't been able to shake the feeling that the one person he most wanted to share the moment with wasn't there beside him. He and Jess had barely talked after the moment she'd kissed him goodbye. But the thought of her had always been there, like a phantom pain in his chest from the piece of his heart she'd taken with her when she'd left.

Yet, he felt a foolish glimmer of hope still leap inside him, as it always did, when he heard the sound of tires crunching on the gravel road. He turned and saw a blue SUV pull up the long driveway to the cottage. How many times had he stood on this very dock, early in the morning, in the middle of the day and late at night, staring at the sky and missing her? How many times had he heard the phone ring or seen a vehicle pull up the drive and found himself hoping it was her?

The SUV stopped. The scruffy, lanky shape of Seth stepped out of the passenger side and tossed a wave in Travis's direction before the hacker barreled down to the beach, catching Willow and Dominic in a hug as they squealed with joy.

Then the driver's-side door opened.

Jess stepped out and Travis felt his heart freeze as her eyes locked on his face. Somehow she was even more beautiful than he remembered. Her hair was tied back in a braid, with gentle wisps slipping down around her face. The fact that she was wearing tan slacks instead of shorts with her pale blue T-shirt meant this was probably a professional visit instead of a spontaneous vacation. But as he walked up the dock and across the ground toward her, he knew with every beat of his heart that this time he wasn't about to let her go until he'd said what he needed to say.

Their footsteps stopped, barely an arm's length away from each other, and they stood there for a long moment without speaking.

"I came to tell you that the Chimera case has been officially closed," Jess said, skipping straight to the point without a "hello" like they always had back when they'd worked together. "His bank accounts were drained, his associates all turned on him, his mercenaries and employees took pleas, and when he realized just how bad things could be if it went to trial, he cut a deal. He'll be spending the rest of his life behind bars, and no longer has either the means or the clout to get revenge on any of the very many people who put him there. It is now the official opinion of the RCMP that while we recommend you exercise caution, the danger and threat he caused to your life is over."

Relief flooded over him like a wave and yet there was still something he needed to know.

"What do you think I should do now?" he asked.

"Go back to Kilpatrick," she said. "It's your home

and your children's home. It's where you belong. The RCMP will provide you any help you need to relocate your family and make sure you're protected."

His family. The incredible and amazing family that God had given him and yet still seemed incomplete. He took another step toward her and she moved toward him. His fingertips gently brushed against hers and he found himself wishing for a perfect time, place and setting to say the three little words that had been there underneath it all for as long as he could remember.

"Jess, I'm completely in love you," Travis said. "As much as I can't wait to move back to Kilpatrick, and spend the rest of my life being Willow and Dominic's dad, I know my life won't be complete without you."

The happiness that filled her eyes was warm, deep, and felt like home. The fingers on both of her hands looped through his, linking them together. But she didn't answer. She just stood there, looking up at him, like she was waiting on him to say something more.

But what? What else was there to possibly say?

"I don't think I'm ever going to go back into police work," he added, "but I'm happy to advise on cases wherever I can. I think you're an incredible cop and more suited for this work than I've ever been. I think I'm cut out to be the one who has the kind of job that lets him be home with the kids, while you're cut out to be the kind who's out there saving lives and solving cases."

A smile curled the corners of her lips. It was gently teasing and the one he knew he wanted to see every day for the rest of his life.

"What else do you want, Travis?" she asked. "Just come out right out and say it."

He swallowed hard.

"I want to marry you," Travis admitted. "I want you to be my wife, help me raise the kids and have a family with me."

And one day, at the right time and the right place, he hoped with all his heart he'd be in a position to ask her that.

"Yes," Jess said. She pulled her hands from his and slid them around his neck. "I love you, Travis, and I'll marry you."

Something leaped in his heart.

"Really?" he said. "You'll marry me?"

"Yes, really!" She laughed. "I've already been reassigned from my existing job with the RCMP to a more senior consulting-detective role that will allow me to work remotely from Kilpatrick while still doing some traveling to work cases. But I'll no longer be out in the field like I was."

"You changed jobs…" He swallowed hard, lost for words. His arms wrapped around her. "Why?"

"Because I want to marry you, Travis," she said. "I want to raise the kids with you, have a family with you, and be your partner in your life, your family, and home forever. And if you hadn't asked me, I'd have asked you."

Joy filled his heart. He leaned forward. His lips brushed hers gently.

"Daddy Travis!" Willow's voice came from behind him. He pulled back, still cradling Jess in his arms as Willow came running across the ground toward them, followed by a red-faced Seth, Dominic in his arms.

Willow stopped short and crossed her arms. Her lips pursed quizzically. "Why are you cuddling Jess?"

Travis laughed. "Because she's going to marry me, and we're all going to live together as a family. What do you say to that?"

Willow paused for a moment and then nodded her approval.

"Okay," she said. "I like that."

Travis laughed. "I like that, too."

Very, very much. More than he had words to say.

"Seth said my book is fiffy towns of 'spensive," Willow said seriously. "But I tol' him it's mine and Dominic's."

Travis glanced at Seth and felt his eyebrows rise. He and Seth had searched the book, inside and out, in the days following Alvin's arrest and had not been able to find any reason why anyone would kill for it.

"Took me a while," Seth said. "But I finally found out why Alvin went through that whole Shiny Man scheme to try to get his hands on Willow and Dominic's bedtime storybook. It's a rare first edition with the unique error of being stitched upside down. It's valued anywhere from fifty to seventy-five thousand dollars."

Travis felt his eyes widen. He fought the urge to whistle.

"But it's mine and Dominic's!" Willow said firmly. "I bought it with my own money!"

Travis nodded. "Yes, it's yours and Dominic's. And we're going to get a very special box with a combination lock to keep it in until you and Dominic are old enough to decide what to do with it. Okay?"

Willow paused a moment. Then nodded and smiled. "Okay."

"Now—" Travis glanced at Seth "—give Jess and me a moment? Then we'll all go talk to Patricia together."

Seth glanced at Jess and nodded. Then the hacker took Willow by the hand and led her up to where Patricia sat on the porch.

"Willow has taken that book out on the motorboat at least twice this summer," Travis said. "And left it on the grass overnight. Thankfully it never got rained on or fell in the lake. I can't believe we had something that valuable in our hands this whole time and didn't see it." Jess chuckled and he laughed, too. "Yeah, I get the irony."

"Sounds like Willow and Dominic have quite the little nest egg for their future," she said.

"Apparently," Travis said.

He glanced to where his adopted family now gathered on the porch. Then he looked back down at the beautiful woman in his arms. Jess's lips brushed his and he lifted her up off her feet as he kissed her back, knowing that in her he'd found all the treasure he'd ever need.

* * * * *

If you enjoyed this story, look for these other books in the Protected Identities series by Maggie K. Black:
Christmas Witness Protection
Runaway Witness

Dear Reader,

When *Rescuing His Secret Child* came out, I got a lot of letters from readers about my valiant little soldier, five-year-old Zander. They were really wonderful to read and I wish I had space here to answer them all. I'm sorry I couldn't find a way to sneak Zander into this book, but as his daddy Nick reports, he now has a little sister.

Many of you asked how I'd come up with Zander. Well, my secret writing weapon is my twelve-year-old daughter. She was only six weeks old when I sold my very first book and grew up watching me write around her. She has a brilliantly creative mind and is one of the very best people to bounce ideas off of.

She helped name baby Fitz from *The Littlest Target* and Eve from *Protective Measures*, and it was her idea for K-9 dog Queenie to play "doggie doggie who's got the phone?" in *Standing Fast*. For this book, I asked her to help me invent another child character and so Willow was created.

I hope one day she writes her own stories.

Thank you again for all of your amazing letters. They encourage me so much and spark so many wonderful ideas. You can message me online at www.maggiekblack.com or find me on Facebook and Twitter under MaggieKBlack.

Thank you for sharing this journey with me.
Mags

*They must work together to solve a cold case...
and to stay alive.*

Read on for a sneak preview of
Deadly Connection *by Lenora Worth,*
the next book in the True Blue K-9 Unit: Brooklyn *series,*
available June 2020 from Love Inspired Suspense.

Brooklyn K-9 Unit officer Belle Montera glanced back on the shortcut through Cadman Plaza Park, her K-9 partner, Justice, a sleek German shepherd, moving ahead of her as she held tightly to his leash. She had a weird sense she was being followed, but it had to be nothing.

Justice lifted his black nose and sniffed the humid air, then gave a soft woof. He might have seen a squirrel frolicking in the tall oaks, or he could have sensed Belle's agitation. Still on duty, she kept a keen eye on her surroundings.

"No time to go after innocent squirrels," she told Justice. "We're working, remember?"

Her faithful companion gave her a dark-eyed stare, his black K-9 unit protective vest cinched around his firm belly.

They were both on high alert.

"It's okay, boy," she said, giving Justice's shiny black-and-tan coat a soft rub. "Just my overactive imagination getting the best of me."

She had a meeting with a man who could have information regarding the McGregor murders. The DNA match from that case had indicated that US marshal Emmett Gage could be related to the killer.

The team had done a thorough background check on the marshal to eliminate him as a suspect, then Belle had been assigned to meet with him.

Justice lifted his head and sniffed again, his nose in the air. The big dog glanced back. Belle checked over her shoulder.

No one there.

She slowed and listened to hear if any footsteps hit the strip of pavement curving through the path toward the federal courthouse near the park.

Belle heard through the trees what sounded like a motorcycle revving, then nothing but the birds chirping. Minutes passed and then she heard a noise on the path, the crackle of a twig breaking, the slight shift of shoes hitting asphalt, a whiff of stale body odor wafting through the air. The hair on the back of her neck stood up and Belle knew then.

Someone is following me.

Don't miss
Deadly Connection *by Lenora Worth,*
available June 2020 wherever
Love Inspired Suspense books and ebooks are sold.

LoveInspired.com

Get 4 FREE REWARDS!

We'll send you 2 FREE Books plus 2 FREE Mystery Gifts.

Love Inspired Suspense books showcase how courage and optimism unite in stories of faith and love in the face of danger.

FREE
Value Over **$20**